A Troubled Heart

Tricia McGill

Print ISBNs
Amazon print 978-0-2286-2857-6
Ingram Spark 978-0-2286-2859-0
BWL Print 978-0-2286-2858-3

Copyright 2023 by Tricia McGill
Cover art by Pandora Designs

of this book.

Table of Contents

Chapter One
Port Arthur Tasmania 1848

Through a haze he could hear a voice somewhere above him, and although vaguely aware that someone had called his name all else was lost in pain. The sweat on his face began to sizzle with the heat—or so it seemed. As he opened his eyes a fraction of this sweat ran into their corners and began to sting as if boiling his eyeballs to add to the sawdust already there, or perhaps it was blood.

"Hang on Finn, yer silly bugger, they've gone to fetch 'elp." The speaker then disappeared and Finn tried to move, but he had to grit his teeth as a searing pain shot through his shoulder and down his arm.

Heaven knew, he'd had his share of agony and discomfort since coming to this godawful place, but this topped it for certain. To take his mind off it he tried to think of better moments in his life, but they were sparce, far back and almost all lost in time.

A sudden movement beside him in the sawpit alerted him that someone had jumped into the pit and was now leaning over him in the narrow space. "Well, here's a fine mess you've got yourself into young fellow," a kindly voice said. "How in heaven did you manage to do this to yourself? They said you was the top man, so how come you ended up down here amid the sawdust and dirt?" Patting Finn on the unhurt shoulder, he added, "I'm what's the nearest to what can be called a doctor here today, they call me Johnson."

Finn squinted up to see that this Johnson was not a lot older than himself, and was likely nearing his thirtieth year. His mop of unruly hair drooped over his forehead as he began to use a knife to hack his way through Finn's shirt sleeve, and Finn gritted his teeth as the pain seemed to worsen. To add to his injury was the knowledge that he'd done this damage by his own foolishness. If he hadn't been larking about as usual to show how handy he was with his fists, none of this would have come about. Never one to shirk from a fight, when the big oaf they called Bear started to taunt him, of course he could not back down from the inevitable.

"You've lost a small amount of blood from your forehead, but as far as I can see it's just where you caught the log on your way down." Turning to rummage about in a small bag he had at his side this Johnson fellow produced a piece of rag and then began to wipe away at the blood. "I fear the problem with your arm could be a lot worse—probably broken." The searing pain when he moved that arm made Finn flinch and Johnson apologised. "It's as I expected, we'll have to get you off to the infirmary." Patting Finn's shoulder he said with a small laugh, "This'll stop you fighting for a while," then apologised again, adding, "Sorry, my attempt at humour."

As another shape appeared above him Finn recognised it as his Scottish working mate Spence who then dropped down to stand at his side opposite the man tending him. "We'll have to haul you up, matey, so grit yer teeth, eh?" Finn's teeth ached already with the gritting. "How the bloody hell you managed to get yourself in this mess, I can't work out. It's not as if you don't know how to look after yourself. Mucking about never did you any good, and if I told you once I told you a million times, stick to the rules."

"'Twas that big oaf Bear, if he hadn't delivered that mighty punch that knocked me sideways and down here, I would have beaten him to next week. Doc here says it's not that bad—that's right isn't it, doc?" Finn grimaced as he tried to push himself up onto his good elbow.

"Well, honestly, I've seen many worse. You were unfortunate that you didn't pick a more suitable spot for your match."

Someone up above then tossed a rope down, ordering, "Tie it round his shoulders, Spence, and we'll haul him up."

Finn had a feeling he might have passed out as he was dragged up out of the pit, only just being squeezed past the huge log that they had been in the process of sawing through when the accident happened. "Guess it could have been worse, matey—if the log had fallen in on top of yer," one of the haulers said as they lay him down beside the pit.

This cheerful observation accompanied by a chuckle did nothing to ease the guilt Finn felt. If they had been working on this one for longer and had cut further through it, the log would have fallen onto Spence, and his mate would not now be alive and kicking. He could only offer thanks that they had only started sawing a short time before his silly argument with Bear. Cursing his idiocy for allowing the big idiot to stir him so, he vowed never to be so daft next time.

As Johnson gave orders for Finn to be assisted to the small cart that stood a short distance away, Finn saw Bear standing some distance back laughing his stupid head off and Finn knew his vow would never be kept.

"How long before I can get back to work, Doc?" he asked, as Johnson clicked the horse into a walk, once he'd ensured Finn was comfortably settled behind him.

Johnson laughed. "In a hurry to get back to the job, are you? I would have thought you would welcome a stay in hospital to get away from the horrible tasks set upon you?"

"Oh, it's not so bad working out here amid the trees, a lot better than working on the new prison they are building." There were times when Finn almost relished the tough going. "It beats the work we were set to up north by a long way, or working on the treadmill all day."

"You came down from Sydney Town, did you, when they decided to close it?"

"Yes, and it won't be long afore I will be a free man. Done my ten years haven't I?"

"Goodness, ten, eh? You must have been a young 'un when they sent you here."

Finn chuckled. "That's a fact. Think I was about fifteen. Never know for sure as I wasn't certain when I was born."

"You aren't alone in that fact, Finn, many of the men in the prison yonder would have no idea when they were brought into this world. One good thing about it is you never have a birthdate to celebrate so don't notice the years passing."

Finn said nothing to that as Johnson pulled the horse up in front of the hospital. No doubt this man had never been locked away in pitch black solitude where all you had to do was count the hours and the minutes as they ticked away. Johnson jumped down, and awkwardly Finn did the same. Together they walked towards the brick structure that Finn thought was one of the ugliest buildings he had ever seen. The pain in his arm had subsided and only ached when he moved it, but he wasn't about to say anything as a night in hospital as the doc said would not be hard to take. Anything was better than sleeping amid the stench of the other men he usually shared his sleeping quarters with.

"I'll leave you here with this capable young man," Johnson said after he'd explained to the fellow who met them as they came in just what he thought was Finn's injury. With a small salute he walked off.

"Can you write?" the man who was some sort of nurse or orderly asked, after he'd led Finn into a room and told him to sit down.

"Yes, I can." Finn felt quite indignant. Being treated like a child irked him. "I've been reading and writing since I was this high." He signaled a spot about knee high. That wasn't strictly true for he hadn't properly learned his letters until he was likely ten or more.

"Write your name here, then." The orderly pointed to the page lying on a table. "What's your sentence? Got much longer to serve, have you?"

"My time is just about up." Finn squared his shoulders, and a twinge of pain reminded him why he was here. "Should get my pardon any day now."

"Right ho." The fellow peered down at the sheet of paper. "Finn O'Connor, you wait here and someone will come along and see what needs to be done." As Finn sat on a bench, he walked out carrying the page.

The next day Finn walked out of the hospital with the proof that he was a free man tucked firmly into his trouser pocket. As luck would have it the injury had turned out to be not broken, but something to do with the shoulder joint having to be pushed back into its rightful position. The doctor who did this told him he had dislocated it when he fell. After the pain from that subsided, he was told to rest it as much as possible. So, no more fighting for some time, was the order given him.

It appeared that when his name came before the Commissariat's office, they realised that his ten-year sentence ended a month or so back and therefore he was deemed free to go wherever he wanted. Just one thing held him back, he had not one penny to his name and possessed just the rags that he stood up in. A young nurse had found him a shirt somewhere to replace the one the doc cut about, but it was not a lot better than the old one. There was the bundle he carried that contained his mug and plate, a worn hairbrush he'd taken from a man who died, and a picture Finn collected somewhere along the way of a place in Ireland called Kilmallock that he kept, as it looked like a nice place to live.

As he pondered what to do next, a soft mutter of annoyance came from behind him and he turned in time to see a woman take a tumble. Landing in a heap at the foot of the steps, her skirts flew about, showing a glimpse of one perfectly shaped ankle. Seldom did females of good breeding travel about alone in these parts so he looked about to see if her carriage driver was here to assist her. A small cart stood not far away, but there was no one else in sight so he went to kneel at her side, asking, "Are you all right miss?"

With a small toss of the head, she looked up at him from the most beautiful pair of eyes he had ever seen. Hair as black as night was pulled back into some sort of roll behind her head beneath the bonnet that she hastily straightened. At a guess he thought perhaps she was about twenty years of age. Not used to being this close to a woman in some time he stood hurriedly and offered a hand, feeling like the idiot he knew she must think him, while he sent up a small prayer of thanks that at least the hand was cleaner than it had been yesterday.

As she took the outstretched hand she smiled, and Finn's silly heart seemed to do a somersault. "Just feeling a bit stupid," she said in what Finn called a posh English accent. "I wasn't looking where I was going."

When she stood—close enough for him to feel her sweet breath on his face, he realised he still held her hand and dropped it as if it was a piece of hot coal. "Easily done," he muttered, looking about again as he asked, "Is your driver somewhere?" again feeling foolish for obviously nobody else was nearby.

"No, I came alone." Holding a small package aloft she added, "Simply came along to pick up this medication for the small girl who is in my charge." Brushing at her skirts, she looked around. "Are you waiting on someone?"

"No, I have just come from the infirmary too—only this was because in my foolishness I had a fall and injured my shoulder." Lifting this arm as if to prove it was also all right, he dropped it swiftly, not knowing what to do or say next, and asked, "Might I ask why you are not afraid of me, Miss? Most females might be inclined to run swiftly from a man alone in these parts." A stupid blush rushed to his cheeks and he cursed his fair skin and light hair, not for the first time, as he turned away in the hope of hiding his face.

At her small laugh he turned back. "Exactly that, sir, you are alone, and I know that had you been a criminal you would most likely have been on the way back to the prison accompanied by a guard—am I correct?"

Finn stared at her. No females that he had come into contact with—and they were few and far between—had been anything like this one. "I've just gained my freedom, Miss, and am wondering where to go and what to do." Feeling the need to prove the truth of this he delved into his pocket and brought out the precious paper and held it aloft.

With barely a glance at it, she laughed again and asked, "So where do you think you will decide on? It's a long trek to Hobart where most seem to head once gaining their release."

Another surprising statement from her. Pushing the paper back into his pocket, he glanced about. "I doubt my meagre funds will take me as far as Hobart at this time— perhaps later. I need to find employment first and foremost."

"Ah, yes." With a finger to her chin, she appeared to be making a decision before she said, "The family I am employed by are in need of a man capable of doing a variety of jobs around their small property, perhaps that would suit. The husband is away a lot about his business and his wife sadly hit a decline after giving birth, and therefore is scared of going out and about, so you would have to prove you are trustworthy."

"And how would I do that, Miss? It's a fact that we are not given a recommendation on receiving our freedom."

With a twist of the mouth as if indicating that she was thinking about that, she looked him up and down before saying, "I will vouch for you. Sadly, your clothing gives away the fact that you have been a convict." Shaking her head she added, "I have an idea. We will soon find a solution to that."

Mystified that a complete stranger—and a female at that—should be so trusting, he blurted, "I could be a murderer for all you know. Why would you help me in this way?"

"I hope I am a good judge of character, and I know a bit about the past of most who gain their freedom. My Papa was a medical man. We relocated here to Port Arthur in forty-five after the hospital was built and he told me tales of men who were transported for the silliest of crimes. So, what was your crime? Steal a loaf of bread did you, or something just as trifling?" Without waiting for his response, she turned and with a wave of the hand said, "Look, I have to get back or my mistress will start panicking, so are you interested or not?" She headed towards the cart, where the horse was in the middle of a nap, its head bent.

Shaking his head in disbelief, Finn trailed after her. Surely this young female was perhaps mad or was she a gift from the gods? Without assistance she climbed aboard the small vehicle and picked up the reins as she sat back on the bench. As he joined her, she asked, "So what name do you go by? Mine's Esther by the way."

"Pleased to meet you, Esther." With a feeling he had drifted into some strange other world, he added, "I go by Finn O'Connor." The Finn part was probably fact. As for his surname, he had no idea who had called him that somewhere along the way in his growing years, but he kept it as a way to prove that he was born in Ireland. As the horse began to trot, he asked, "You said your Pa was a medical man—is he not one anymore?"

"Sadly, for me, my dear Papa, along with my Mama, was killed just last year when the carriage they were in overturned after hitting a rock."

"Oh, I am sorry to hear that. It must have been awful for you. Are you alone now or do you have siblings?"

After a deep sigh, she admitted, "It was the worst time of my life—and no I have no brothers or sisters. That of course is why I am employed as companion of sorts to the girl in need of the medication I was sent to collect. It's a shame, but she is currently a sickly child and has a nasty cough."

"So, you not only lost your parents, you also lost your home?" Although he had never known what it was to have a real family, nonetheless a place somewhere near Finn's heart ached for this young girl who had hers snatched away so cruelly.

Without answering that, she gestured ahead to where a cottage surrounded by a few trees sat atop a slight knoll. "We have arrived," she said as she pulled up a short distance from a gate in the fence surrounding the garden. "Say little to my mistress, but let me explain to her that you are looking for employment." Finn nodded, still feeling as if he was in the middle of some strange dream. "Please wait here while I go and fetch you something more presentable to wear. I suppose you realise that you look far worse than a farmer's scarecrow in those filthy rags." The look of scorn she sent to his trousers made him realise such if her words had not.

As she walked off, he scratched at his head, knowing at least his hair and body were now clean after the nights' stay in the infirmary. Was there no end to the oddness of this female? Where on earth would she find clothing for him? Surely not from her employer's wardrobe?

And how could she be so trusting of a complete stranger and an ex-con at that. If he found the will to do it, he could jump onto her cart and urge the horse away as fast as it could go. Common sense kicked in just as fast as that idea hit him—the troopers would be after him in no time and it was doubtful if the guards would let him pass the place called Eaglehawk Neck anyway, where it was rumoured they kept starving dogs tethered, not to mention the guards who were reported to be no better than savages. And with no money or chance to earn some, about the only option available would be to join up with a gang of bushrangers or the like.

Then there was the matter of this girl who was close to being the best person he had ever come across. She soon returned as he stood rubbing the soft nose of the horse whose warm breath was strangely comforting. Pressing the bundle she held beneath her arm into Finn's arms, she advised, "Go behind that tree and change, then wait for my return." Speechless he obeyed, watching her as she led the horse around the fence, disappearing behind the house.

The trousers were of good quality, and she had even provided him with an undergarment such as he had never worn in all his adult years. The shirt he tucked into the belt of these trousers felt soft as butterfly wings against his skin. Lastly, he pulled on a waistcoat, just as she called out, "Are you ready?"

Picking up his ragged trousers and holey shirt he rolled them into a ball before going to stand before her. "I have to ask you, miss, whose togs do I have the pleasure of wearing?"

Sucking her bottom lip in she nodded as she ran her eyes up and down his length. "They were my Pa's. As luck would have it, I was loathe to part with all of my parents' belongings after their unfortunate death. I am happy that they fit you well. My Papa was also a big man." Turning abruptly, she waved over her shoulder. "Come, we will go and present you to my mistress. Leave your discarded things there beneath that tree and you can burn them later." Stopping before the doorway she said, "I unfortunately have no boots that I could get for you."

"That's fine. I got these from a bloke who lost a bet not too long ago." Truth was the fellow who owned them died, and Finn had to fight a couple of the other men who were set on getting them.

"I told my mistress that I met you on the road. Say that you are seeking work and can do most jobs around the house and outside. Do not mention that you have only recently been given your freedom."

As he followed her, Finn took in the house before them. By no means a rich man's property, it was a sturdy cottage which he presumed had been provided for the master of the house on coming to take up his post in the area, whatever that was. As they went beneath the small porch and through the doorway, the smell of cooking coming from somewhere at the back of the house was welcoming and his mouth watered as the thought of a good home-cooked meal made him glad this girl had brought him here, if nothing else mapped out.

A small girl came from one of the rooms and eyed him warily as she demanded, "Who's that?"

"Now Becky, don't be rude, I taught you better manners than that. This is Finn and he is going to work for your Mama." Wrinkling her tiny nose, the child sent Finn a frown before following his rescuer through a doorway.

A long time had passed since Finn stood inside such a building, in fact the courthouse where his sentence was announced those ten years ago was the last place where he'd come up against members of the gentry. It was obvious by the scant furnishings that these people could not be termed nobs though. Digging his hands into the trouser pockets he felt a sense of elation such as he'd never felt in his life. From convict and inmate of the devil's own prison to an almost employed worker—and all within a matter of a day. What would Spence have to say about this kettle of fish when next he saw him?

When Esther appeared at the doorway beckoning him, he straightened his spine before following her. The woman who reclined on a sofa took him by surprise. Fully expecting a dowdy older person, she was almost beautiful, and not a lot older than himself. Hair the colour of sand was drawn back from a narrow face. Sad eyes took in his entire length from his unruly hair to his battered boots, before she said, "Esther tells me that you are handy around the house and garden, is that so?"

Deciding to be on his best behaviour, he gave her a small bow before answering, "Yes Ma'am, I can put my hand to just about anything." Spence would laugh heartily at that lie.

With a small nod, she asked, "So why are you seeking employment with us? Did your previous employer not want your services anymore, and if that were the case, just why was that so if you are so handy?" This was said with a touch of what he thought was derision.

Glancing at Esther in confusion, he realised that he had not taken the time to concoct a story that might please this woman. She came to his rescue by saying, "Finn's previous employer recently went back to England."

The woman nodded as she continued to stare at him. As if coming to a decision she said, "I will not tolerate alcohol consumption of any kind while you are in our employ, is that understood? My husband will decide on a wage—if any is earned, and if you prove worthless then you will leave without causing us any fuss or bother."

Finn nodded, while thinking how odd this person seemed to be—but then again what did he know about the upper class except they could be bullies and tyrants. "Thank you, Ma'am, I vow to do my very best." Inside he wondered how good his best would be. And then wondered if his rescuer Esther was by now likely regretting her rash decision to fetch him here. Following on from that was the question once again of why she had been so keen to bring him here.

With a flap of the hand his new employer said, "Take him to the stable Esther, where he can sleep. He can come to the kitchen at meal times where Nelly will give him food. The only time you are to come into the house...Finn...is if we need you for heavy work that the women cannot undertake, such as bringing logs for the fire." As if suddenly coming to a thought, she added, "And do not pay attention to our silly maid Cora who is likely to desire your interest." She rubbed at her head then as if it was paining her, and flapped her hand again in dismissal.

Esther nodded to Finn and he followed her out, feeling the need to rub at his own head in total confusion. The child tagged behind them as he followed Esther around the house to what Finn presumed was the stable. "Mama doesn't like you much," the girl informed him, adding, "But I think you are probably nice—you have a funny name though."

"Ah, that's because it's Irish, and I am glad you like me," Finn said, feeling so odd he wondered how many other peculiar folks he would find dwelling in this house. Esther seemed to be the most sensible, but following on from that thought came the one that perhaps she wasn't or why else would she have picked up a likely convict and decided to assist him in this way.

The girl skipped ahead to where the horse still stood harnessed to the cart in front of the shed which consisted of an open section where there was space for two vehicles. "Once you get settled, could you please take care of removing my horse's harness, Finn." Stroking the bay's head she said, "Danny Boy here is of Irish descent much like yourself. Everything goes in there." She pointed to the open part where, apart from a few bales of hay, there was a jumble of odd pieces of equipment including a chopper and a handsaw. "Come, I will show you where you can make yourself comfortable. I did not think it through when I invited you along, but the cook Nelly and the maid Cora sleep yonder there in the small room alongside the laundry." Her gesture took in a small addition tagged onto the back of the cottage. "It is a small residence without room for staff."

"Esther sleeps in my room," the child informed him before coughing a few times and then skipping off back towards the house—obviously tired of this new addition to the household.

"She doesn't seem to be so sickly," Finn said, thinking that she appeared to be quite lively—as compared to some of the very poorly kids he had lived amongst in his early days before his capture.

"Her cough mostly bothers her at night, upsetting her Mama," Esther said before opening the door to one side of the shed.

Finn followed her inside to where it smelt strongly of horse and hay. Surprisingly, the space was larger than he expected. A roped off section was no doubt where two horses could be settled at night, and he wondered briefly where he could sleep. Esther answered that when she pointed to what was no more than a rough shelf, saying, "There is a cot of sorts where you can make yourself comfortable. At least it is closed off from the weather. I am afraid you will have to share it with Danny and the master's horse and their hay and grain. Perhaps you can stuff some straw into a grain sack to make a mattress of sorts. I will see what I can fetch you for bed coverings and perhaps find you some other items of clothing."

As if thinking this over, she turned saying, "I will leave you to take care of Danny. Once unharnessed he goes into the small yard until nightfall—there behind the shed. The master's horse goes straight into his stall when he gets home, which is usually at a late hour." After a quick jab in that direction, she began to walk off.

"Can I ask you one question before you go," Finn called after her. When she stopped and faced him, he asked, "Just why are you doing this for a man who for all intents could be a rogue and a thief?"

Sending him a smile, she surprised him once again by saying, "My father taught me not to judge a person by their past, Finn. Use your intuition he advised, for there are many types of men here in the colonies, and you will learn that not always those who are incarcerated for so-called criminal offences are the untrustworthy ones." While he stared at such wise words from one so young, she added, "Do not prove my judgement wrong, will you?" With a small nod she walked away.

Chapter Two

Esther sat on the side of her bed brushing her hair, while she contemplated her perhaps stupid actions of the day. What had she been thinking? Inside, something told her that bringing Finn O'Connor here might turn out to be the most impulsive action of her life. "Oh Papa, please tell me I did the right and Christian thing," she whispered. After plaiting her thick and sometimes tiresome hair that now reached almost to her waist, she pulled the coverlet over her and let out a sigh.

Becky stirred and mumbled in her sleep before turning over. The night promised to be hot, and Esther felt a restlessness such as never before, but felt sure it had nothing to do with the heat. Something about the stranger she had felt compelled to assist had awakened certain unknown feelings within her. How she wished Mama was here—she would offer wise advice. How stupid, for if Mama were still alive, she would not be living in this house, caring for a child and the girl's feckless mother. Letting out a small sob of self-pity, she turned onto her side and stared into the darkness as she not for the first time tried to block out the horror of the day when both beloved parents left this world.

A small tap on her shoulder brought Esther out of a light sleep. Becky stood so close to her she could feel her breath on her face. "I have to wee," she said grumpily.

Esther sighed. "Use the chamber pot. You are not a baby any more, Becky, and are capable of managing on your own."

"Can't see it, it's too dark." Her complaint was followed by a cough and a few sniffles. As always, she made a drama out of the smallest task.

"It is not dark at all for the moon is bright tonight and there is plenty of light coming through the window."

"I'm scared of that Finn man, he might come into our room and hurt us."

"Oh Becky, do not be silly—he is a kind man and will not harm us, and I distinctly remember that you said you liked him." As she said that, Esther wondered just why she felt so sure that he was kind and would not hurt them. Free man he might be, but until only recently he had been locked away amid thugs and ne'er do wells, and for all she knew he had been sent there for committing some horrendous crime.

With a small harrumph Becky took care of her problem and climbed back into her small cot. Esther got up and went over to the window. The moon was so bright that she could clearly see the man who had kept her from her slumber standing over by the fence around the small paddock, and he was stroking Danny Boy's head. They had decided to let the horse stay outside as it was such a warm night.

Later, she would ask herself just why she felt the need to slip into her shoes and with great stealth leave the room. The small wind that blew in from the sea was cool upon her face as she went across to stand at the man's side. She was not small by any means but she came just about to his shoulder. Danny Boy snickered and put his muzzle close to her face, breathing softly onto her cheek. A few moments passed before the man called Finn said softly, "Could not sleep either eh, Miss?"

"'Tis fair hot. I often have trouble sleeping since my parents died. What about you? Was the cot allocated to you so uncomfortable?"

As he looked down on her for the first time, she recalled that she had left the house in her nightgown, and her cheeks burned as she wondered what had prompted her to come outside almost unclothed. Fighting an urge to run, she crossed her arms across her breasts, realising that they suddenly felt unusually heavy.

"I've slept in worse beds, believe me Esther. There is little wrong with this one." He jerked his head in the direction of the stable.

"Did you not have a comfortable bed to sleep on in the days before your arrest? What about your childhood?"

With a small laugh he shook his head. "My childhood was to say the least a sketchy one. Mind you, I only recall a small amount of the tales related to me and have no idea if they were made up or not."

Intrigued now, she forgot her embarrassment and asked, "You did not spend your childhood with your Ma and Pa?"

His small laugh announced how ridiculous that thought was. "I have no idea who fathered me, but I was told that my Ma died not long after my birth and along came a gypsy who took me as her own."

Esther let out a small gasp. "And this gypsy woman then brought you up?"

"Far from it. I think I was going on two when some fancy English woman who was passing through Kilmallock with her nob of a husband decided it was no fit life for a child, and she more or less stole me away and that is how I ended up in London.”

“Goodness me, I cannot believe that she could simply whisk you away like that. Were there no laws for such abduction?”

“Oh, there were laws for the rich and noble but not for us common Irish folk.” With a shrug he patted Danny Boy’s head. “Thinking back on it, I suppose they thought they were offering me a better life.”

“And they were not?” To Esther his was a sorry tale, which left her thinking that he was probably destined for a life of crime from an early age. “And so, you resided in their house in London?”

His laugh came out as more of a soft grunt than one of humour. “And what a right disaster that was. Their two stuck up daughters hated the fact that I was allowed to sit in on their lessons, and their merry tantrums meant I barely learned more than how to add one and two together.”

“Poor man. But you must have at least learnt to read and write?” Feeling quite bewildered at such treatment that was so far removed from her own childhood, her heart ached for the boy that he was.

“Not at all. I was in about my tenth year when I could stand it no more and fled in the dark of night, taking little but the clothes I wore and a couple of their books."

"But where did you go. I cannot for one moment imagine how a ten-year-old would manage to survive alone in a city."

"I wasn't alone for long, Miss, for there were many boys who lived a life on the streets of London, so in no time I had what I considered my family. There were about six of us, and we survived mostly on our wits— and thieving of course. The biggest who we thought of as our leader, well he taught me how to read and write."

It was taking Esther some time to digest all this. About to say something more, the jingle of harness warned of an approaching vehicle. Startled she cried, "I must get back to my bed. The master of the house is coming. He may need assistance with his horse. Tell him only what you told the mistress. Oh, and go to the kitchen at dawn for your breakfast." Leaving him standing there she fled as fast as she could, thankful she could get inside the house through the kitchen entrance.

Her employer often returned late at night, and usually took care of unharnessing his gelding. Esther stood by her window watching as the two men faced each other, obviously discussing who Finn was and what he was doing here, then the master strode to the house, and Esther climbed into bed knowing what was coming.

The mistress's shrill cry of, "Why are you so late again?" did not surprise Esther, for he was always greeted in this way. The soft thud of their bedroom door told her he had gone into their room, and then in a loud voice he demanded why she had seen fit to take on some character who could likely be a criminal. For some time, all Esther could hear was his loud rumble and his wife's soft cries and pleas.

How Esther dreaded ending up in such a relationship—and hoped sincerely she could find a man to offer her a love such as her parents shared. Her Papa was such a patient soul and treated his wife as an equal, for she was just as clever as he. Both of them instilled a compassion in Esther for those less fortunate.

Finn's story took up all her thoughts for some time and when Becky shook her shoulder imploring her to wake up, it was with heavy eyes she looked up at the girl who stood coughing into her palm. "I am sorry, Becky I was dreaming. Go fetch your medicine." As she put her feet to the floor, a soft knock announced that Cora had brought their water for washing.

"Morning Miss," the maid chirped as she placed the ewer on the small dressing table.

"Master's gone off already." Leaning closer to Esther she said in a near whisper, "Right barney they were having when I took their breakfast in earlier. Did you hear it?" Cora liked nothing better than a gossip.

"No, I did not hear it, and you should be more aware that what they do or say is not your business."

Her reprimand was shrugged off by the maid who went on, "He don't seem too happy about the new help—even though I see that Finn had his horse all harnessed and ready to go as soon as the sun came up." When she got no response from Esther, she made a face and left.

If Mr. Franklin had already gone about his business, then Esther wondered if he at least had given Nelly instructions on the tasks she could set Finn. Shrugging, she prepared Becky and herself for the day.

Finn was sitting at the table when they went into the kitchen, and Becky went and sat beside him on the bench, staring up at him in curiosity as she asked, "Are you going to stay here or did my Papa tell you to go?"

Esther gave Finn a questioning look before taking the chair opposite him at the table. "Did he?" she queried.

Rubbing his chin, Finn chuckled. "To be honest the man said little, apart from asking where I came from and what I was capable of doing. I set his mind at rest by telling him I was no criminal set on robbing him." With another small chuckle he cleared his bowl of porridge.

Nelly handed Cora a breakfast dish which she then placed on the table in front of Esther before going around and sitting beside Finn, so close that when he tried to move away from her, he was penned in on his other side by Becky who was now spooning up her porridge. Cora placed a hand on his forearm, exclaiming, "You are very strong, I'll bet you can lift anything, would you like to lift me?"

Abruptly Finn rose, shaking free and climbing over the bench as he said, "Best go in now, for Nelly here told me the mistress said I was to see her about what tasks she wanted me to be doing this morning."

Cora watched him with a dreamy look in her eyes until he left the room and then said, "Isn't he handsome?"

"Now now, Cora, keep your foolish thoughts to yourself," Nelly chided as she began to pour water from the huge kettle into the sink. "He's here to work, same as you are, so get on with your chores and stop with your dopey chatter or else I will report you to the mistress. The big carpet in the parlour needs a good brush and then you can make a start on the laundry.”

Cora made a face behind Nelly's back before scurrying off. Nelly turned to Esther and asked, “Where did you find that one?” This was asked with a jerk of the head.

“I met him along the road, Nelly, and as he was looking for work and I knew you needed more help around the place I suggested he try here.” Of course, that was not strictly true, but still Esther could not find a logical excuse for just why she had befriended Finn. After hearing his tale, she felt glad that she had taken a chance on him, for his start in life had been anything but easy if his story was to be believed. “You sorely needed someone to fetch water from the well and take care of the harder tasks needing a man's strength.” Rising, she said, “Come Becky, we must start your lessons. It is a lot cooler today so perhaps we will sit outside. Fetch your chalk and board and we will continue with sums.”

When they were settled beneath the branches of the only tree close to the house, Finn strode towards them and sat beside Esther on the bench. “Your mistress is a rare one for sure, isn't she?” This was said with a nod towards the house.

“I think she is a very miserable person,” Esther said softly. Becky was engrossed in her adding and subtracting tasks that Esther had set her and paid no attention to them. "I should not discuss my employers, but sadly they do not have a contented relationship. Did she give you an idea of what your tasks will be?"

Rubbing at his brow, he said, "Fact is, she was more interested in how I came to meet you and why I was in this part of the country, wanting to know more about me. I'm ashamed to say I lied, telling her that I came over from Ireland only recently." He leant closer and whispered, "Is she slightly mad? Her hands were a-fidgeting all the time, and she seemed to have a need to touch me."

Esther had no idea how to answer that. It had occurred to her early on in her time here that Mrs. Franklin was what her mother would have called unbalanced after the stresses of childbirth. "So, you still do not know what your tasks are?"

"She said to see Nelly, so that is what I shall do." Pressing his hands on his knees he rose. "I'm not sure about the master of the house either. They are an odd pair of sods to be sure. But at least he gave me some idea of what I should start on. I think he was happy with me preparing his horse for the day. I gave the fellow a good brushing."

Esther watched him stride off. Cora was right, he was a very strong and handsome fellow. Hair as light as his was rare for a man, but it suited him. With a slight shake of the head, she realised that she was spending far too much time contemplating what it would be like to be held in those strong arms of his. This would never do—she was becoming as foolish as Cora. "Have you finished yet, Becky?" She took the offered chalk board and was pleased to see that the child was doing well at her sums. "Now, we shall do some reading." Esther took a book of simple rhymes from her basket and patted the bench beside her.

A short time later she saw Finn toting water from the well, obviously on the way to fill the laundry tub for Cora. The girl would no doubt use that opportunity to bother him with her silly nonsense. The sudden burst of jealousy Esther felt made her give herself a shake at the foolishness of that thought.

Chapter Three

With ease, Finn cut through the piece of timber and placed it on top of the small pile that sat ready for patching up the shed where he and the two horses shared their sleeping space. After being used to sawing through the trunks of massive trees, where a gang of usually twenty of more men were needed to carry it from one place to another, this task was almost what he considered child's work.

Taking the kerchief from around his neck he wiped at his face and looked off into the distance. Danny Boy snickered so he walked across to where the horse was standing by the fence. "Hello young fellow, feeling a little down in the dumps, are you?" In response the horse wiggled his head up and down as if answering. "Well, if I had my way I would be on your back now and we would be galloping off over yonder hill."

"Oh, you would, would you?" Finn jumped as he turned to face Esther who stood a few paces away, a mug in her hand. "So, you would ride off forever, stealing my

Danny away?" This was asked with a smile in her voice.

Finn shook his head vigorously. "Oh no, miss, I would not be so horrible after what you have done for me...I didn't mean forever." That was a fact. A few times in the week since she brought him here, he had considered doing just that a few times. The master of the house was rarely home, and the feckless mistress was becoming a nuisance, often scaring him with the way she watched him. Fact was, he felt sure she was more than a little mad, reminding him at times of the silly Englishwoman who took him away from Ireland as a child. He was beginning to understand why the master was never home. With nobody to watch over him, Finn could help himself to many things that he could easily sell in the nearest town, including the horse. Just one thing—or person—kept him here.

Esther handed him the mug and gestured to the nearby log. "Come sit and drink your tea. And don't you think it is about time that you stopped calling me miss and recognised that I have a name? After all, I thought we knew each other better now—I am certainly not your superior, just an employee here as you are."

Oh, he most definitely knew her better. Knew that she had a smile that could make his insides melt like snow in the sun, make him stumble and stutter over his words at times as if he were a stupid boy. And she always smelled as if she had walked through a bed of what he now knew was lavender. When they were seated side by side on the log and her scent drifted about, he swigged the tea down in such a hurry that it caused him to cough. "Beg pardon, miss, er Esther. I was thirsty. Where is the child, Becky? Not sick again, is she?" he asked in a hurry to hide his confusion.

Esther shook her head. "Her Mama has ordered her to bed, against the girl's protests. The poor child still has her troublesome cough, but the mistress ignores my advice that the girl needs fresh air and sunshine, not to be shut up in a darkened room."

"She does know that your Pa was a medical person does she not?" He set the mug near his feet.

"As you have probably concluded by now, the mistress is not a well person, in fact has many problems. She forgets most things." She stood and went across to pat Danny's neck. "How is your own injury? I haven't noticed that it bothers you at all."

Finn joined her at the fence, rubbing at the said shoulder. "To be honest, I have forgotten that it was hurt." But not forgotten how it got injured. He still bore a sense of injustice that he had no chance to ensure that the brute Bear paid for laughing at Finn's misfortune. A chance had not risen since coming here to pay the idiot back for besting him in the fight. Truth was, he had no desire whatever to visit the logging camp.

"Are you happy here, Finn?" she surprised him by asking.

Not about to let her know just how happy simply being in her company made him, he twisted his mouth as if in thought before saying, "I don't have much choice do I miss, er Esther, for where would I go anyway?"

"Don't take me for a fool, Finn, you are a person who has known what it is like to live by your wits, so I am certain you would have no trouble doing just what I heard you say. You could steal away on my horse, taking plenty of things from the house."

"Ah, but how far would I get Esther, afore they were a' chasing after me? I would not be such a fool to think I could even get past Eaglehawk Neck afore they had me back in chains and working on the timber cutting or worse, the treadmill at the granary."

She went back to sit on the log and he joined her. "If I were completely honest, Finn, I sometimes consider doing just what you mentioned. After all, Danny Boy belongs to me so nobody could clamp me in chains for taking him elsewhere. My Papa left me well provided for, so I would never be penniless."

"So, what keeps you here? You could have your choice of places to go to in this massive land."

"Hmm, I suppose what keeps me here is perhaps fear of the unknown. Unlike you, Finn, I have never known what it is to live by my wits—and a female alone attracts all kinds of unwelcome attention. My parents were very protective of me, so no doubt I sought that same type of protectiveness from Mr. and Mrs. Franklin." Her deep sigh showed how disappointing that wish had proved. After another sigh she urged, "Tell me more about your early years Finn. Your life has been so different to mine in every way. I could not imagine going off on my own, or worse, not knowing my own parents."

Looking over at the horse who was now munching at the sparce grass, Finn thought back over his life and the differences. "Well, strange as it may sound, I did have some happy times. When I shared my life with the gang, we got up to some capers I can tell you. Worst part was the hunger I guess—some of the smaller boys weren't up to stealing food so us bigger sods had to look after them."

"Goodness, how did so many younger ones end up living on the streets?" Her face showed her shock.

Finn shook his head. "Their ma's were mostly street women—some got knocked about by their handlers and some could not cope with a kid hanging on their skirts while they went about their business. One tart actually went off and left her little 'un with us telling a tale of having to go visit her family. She never returned."

"How appalling." Esther rubbed at her pink cheek. "I cannot imagine such a life. I suppose I should consider myself fortunate for having a loving family, if only for my growing years." Staring down at her dainty feet she asked, "And how did you end up being captured?"

With a small laugh, Finn said, "Me and this other kid had an idea to get ourselves a goat. We were at the market one day and saw a bloke milking his goat, and we thought it would be a good idea to have fresh milk every day, especially the younger boys. We decided a cow would be too big and might stand out in London more than a goat, so off the pair of us went and walked a fair mile or so one day to where we thought we would find such an animal wandering about. When we saw this creature with another few goats, we thought perhaps no one would miss it, so caught it with the rope we had thought to bring with us. We would have got away with it too, but we hadn't gone far before this fellow we realised was from a nearby farm came after us with a pitchfork. My partner in crime got a nasty wound in his leg from that weapon, so I stopped to help him. Bad idea as it worked out, for it just happened that the local constable was visiting the farm and we were nabbed then and there."

"Even so, it seemed a measly crime for two lads to end up being transported for, Finn."

"Don't look so down about it, Esther. It had to happen sooner or later for many got nabbed for much lesser crimes. And would you believe we learned that the goat we were after stealing was a Billy and we wouldn't have got much milk from that anyway." Finn laughed, but looking back to that awful time it wasn't so funny back then. "At least the pair of us got sent here together and stayed together until poor old Cal got sickly just afore I got sent south. He never recovered, poor sod."

"And I don't suppose it even occurred to you that the animal has to give birth to a young one to produce milk."

Shaking his head, Finn chuckled. "Course not, we were stupid. After seeing this man milking his goat, we thought we could do that." Rising, he stretched, just as the mistress came towards them at a run, screaming nonsense—a rare sight for she seldom went far from the house.

"Becky is calling for you, Esther, what are you doing out here?" she shouted. With tousled hair and red cheeks from her obvious distress, she looked like the mad woman Finn had suspected her to be. "Get inside and assist the child. I cannot handle her; I was looking everywhere for you and find you dallying here with the help." The look of disdain she shot at Finn would have shrivelled him if he was so inclined.

Without a word Esther walked off. Mona Franklin watched her for a while before turning back to Finn. As if the episode had not occurred, she smiled weirdly at him before saying, "I don't like you spending time with the girl. She is paid to look after my daughter not dally here with you. In future I do not wish you to spend time with her—or silly Cora for that matter."

Ignoring her tirade, Finn went to pick up the saw, bent and carried on with sawing the wood, intent on giving the stupid woman no attention. He'd suffered many a worse telling off in his time. He could feel her gaze on his back for some time before she returned to the house, humming low as she walked. It always puzzled Finn how the folk who had the wealth and security were seemingly the ones who were never satisfied with their lot in life. The master had not returned much before sundown once since Finn came here, and he and the mistress barely exchanged a civil word when he did appear. Finn learned that Mr. Franklin worked for the Government as some sort of ledger keeper so surely that occupation shouldn't keep him away for such long hours. No doubt he had a paramour tucked away—and who could blame him for not wishing to hurry home to his strange wife.

Later that evening when the sun was just about meeting the horizon, Finn went into the kitchen for his supper. Nelly put his plate before him on the table, tutting to herself when the shrill voice of the mistress came to them from her room along the passage. Looking flustered, Cora rushed in and with a huff sat opposite Finn. "What you been doing now, girl?" Nelly asked as she wiped her hands on a cloth that she always carried tucked down her apron.

"I ain't done a thing. She's as mad as a stung cat is that woman. Told me off for nothing, she did. I was only trying to help her on with her nightgown, and she called me a name I shan't repeat." She dipped a chunk of bread into the stew that Nelly set in front of her. Giving Finn a wink she said low, "If you ever think of getting away from this loony bin, I'll come with you."

Finn ignored her remark, and carried on eating as he wondered where Esther was. When she did come in shortly after Cora, he heard her say low to cook, "I fear the mistress is worsening each day, Nelly. If only her husband were here more, she might calm down. Her tantrums are affecting the child— poor Becky is constantly asking me why her Mama hates her so."

He could not hear Nelly's response to that, and when Esther sat beside him, she shook her head before picking up her soup spoon. They ate in silence for a while, and when thunder rumbled across the sky, Finn rose, saying, "I will fetch Danny in before the rain starts."

He had barely settled the horse inside and given him a handful of grain before the skies opened. It was still pelting down heavily when the master came home, so Finn pulled a grain sack over his head and shoulders and went outside. Without a word of greeting Mr. Franklin marched off, leaving Finn to remove the harness and settle both horse and small cart inside.

Lighting the candle inside the small lantern that Esther ensured he had, Finn stripped off his now wet breeches and shirt and pulled on the other shirt she'd given him, and with nothing left to do but settle down for the night, he took out the small book that he treasured. "I'm sorry, as it is probably not to your liking but apart from my Papa's medical books, I have nothing else that might interest you," Esther had said when she gave it to him.

The book contained drawings of animals that could be found in this area with explanations of their habits. Some of the words were very long and Finn had no idea what most of them meant, but hoped that when Esther had the time, she might explain their meaning to him. Barely had he sat back and opened to the page he had reached, when a shrill scream echoed from the direction of the house.

Jerking up, he pulled on his breeches with haste and then his boots. Even as he opened the door screams still rang out. Rain splattered his face as he ran towards the kitchen door. As he went inside it was clear that the screams were coming from the mistress of the house. The kitchen was empty, and in between screams she also yelled words that Finn had only heard previously from fellow inmates and scoundrels on the streets, forcing him to wonder where she had learnt such language. Fearing the worst, he headed along the passage towards the din.

Cora stood by the open door, and he could see by the lantern she held aloft that her face bore shock and horror. Nelly stood beside her mistress trying in vain to quieten her, while Esther knelt at the side of the master, who lay on his back covered in more blood than Finn had ever seen pour from one human—blood that spurted from a wound made by the blade sticking out of his chest. As she saw him, Esther cried, "He is dead, Finn, what shall we do?"

Finn's first thought was to get her away from the body. Already her hands and arms were splattered with blood. Only then did he notice the child Becky shrunk into a corner of the room, hands over her ears. "Get the girl out of here, Esther," he urged as he tugged on her arm.

As if suddenly realising that the child was there and whimpering, Esther rose and went to her. It took her a few tugs before Becky suddenly jumped up and ran full pelt out of the room, Esther at her heels. Nelly left the mistress's side and came across to say to Finn, "We must inform the constables. Can you ride out and do that?" The cook seemed to be the only one of the women with her wits still about her. Mona Franklin's screams had subsided into small sobs and hiccups.

Nodding his agreement, Finn left her there and went in search of Esther. Following the sound of her soft murmurings, he went through the open door of what was obviously her and the child's bedroom. "Nelly thinks I should fetch the constable,

Esther." As the thought of that task hit home Finn swallowed a feeling of panic. As the only man here available to do the task he knew he must. "Should I take Danny Boy or the master's horse, what do you think?"

Looking up at him with tears streaking down her face, she nodded. "Take the master's bay, Finn. He is bigger and probably speedier." As if pondering on this, she added, "I have a saddle and bridle that my Papa used, but I am not sure if Mr. Franklin's horse is used to the saddle. I have not seen him ridden since coming here." Jumping up she came across to his side, rubbing at her brow. "Do what you feel is best Finn—and thank you. I do not know what I would do if you weren't here to help. The saddle is stored in the big chest in the shed." Shuddering, she looked about forlornly, saying, "What a disaster. I wonder what prompted her to act in such a fashion."

"The woman is not of sound mind, Esther, we shared that thought." Patting her arm, he nodded towards the child, who still whimpered pitifully. "I suggest you bathe her and also clean yourself while I am gone. Nelly can stay with the mistress. And for goodness' sake, calm Cora down." The girl was now wailing in the passageway.

Finn strode past her, wondering as he went outside how things had come to this and also wondered why he hadn't told Esther that he had never been astride a horse in his life. The closest he had come to it was when he and his mates thought it a grand lark once to steal a donkey and take it for a ride. The creature was about knee high to the tallest lad and when Finn cocked his leg over it his feet almost touched the ground. The donkey's owner came out then yelling at them and they all took off at a run.

Standing by the door of the shed he stared at the master's horse who was still standing. Danny was lying down snoring, so it looked as if he would have to ride the bay. Going to the chest that he already knew contained the saddle and other pieces of harness he pulled it out, then the bridle. Pulling on the jacket that Esther had given him on his second day here, he then went over to the bay. It took a few tries before he got the bridle secured, and he said a silent prayer when he placed the saddle cloth over the animals' back, and then the saddle, while the horse thankfully stood calmly. Not having any idea if he was pulling the strap too tightly around the horse's belly, he spoke gently in the hope he did it right. As luck would have it the rain had ceased as he led the horse outside. Plonking his hat firmly on his head he placed his foot in the stirrup and eased himself up into the saddle.

"Come on boy," he encouraged, when the horse made no effort to move. With a few more encouraging words the animal took a few steps but then stopped and bent its head to take a nibble of grass. Finn now had no idea what to do, short of whacking it across the rump, and he admitted to himself that he feared it would then career off at a gallop. He'd seen a few men in his time ill-treating their nags and was not about to do that, but knew he had to do something. Pulling on the reins he at least got its head up, and moving forward slowly.

"At this rate fella, it'll be daybreak before we reach the barracks." As he said that he caught sight of a group of riders ahead. At this time of night, it could possibly be a gang of thieves and scoundrels and now he worried because he had no weapon to protect himself with. The riders were moving at a fair pace and grew near enough for him to realise they were troopers—likely on the lookout for runaways from the prison.

He was just about to hail them when the leading rider yelled, "Stop, who goes there?"

An old feeling of panic surged through him then, but he swallowed it and called out, "Your help is needed sir," feeling that perhaps adding this term of address would help them realise that he was not on the run or a horse thief. "There's been a horrible crime committed. I was on the way to get help."

By now they had pulled their mounts up a few paces away, and he could see there were about six of them. The one he presumed was the leader brought his horse aside Finn's and ordered, "State your name boy, and where this crime has taken place."

While objecting to the man's manner, Finn nonetheless swallowed his inbuilt hatred of the military and said, "I'm Finn O'Connor and work for Mr. Franklin who lives yonder." He turned and pointed to the cottage that he realised he could still make out in the distance, for the sky had cleared somewhat. "Perhaps I should say I worked for him sir, for the man is dead, stabbed by his wife, I fear. As I am the only man working there, I was given the task of fetching help."

"You say Mr. Franklin has been slain. Are you certain that he is dead?" The man obviously knew of the master as he looked taken aback with shock.

"As certain as I could be, for when I left, he had a long blade embedded in his chest, and his wife was covered in his blood."

Turning in his saddle the man shouted, "You Jenkins, Pike and Phipps, get back to headquarters with haste and fetch the constables." He pointed to the cottage asking, "That is where the crime has been committed, young fella?"

"Yes sir."

Once those three galloped off he and the two other troopers followed Finn whose mount moved faster going home than he had moved leaving it, so in no time they were all dismounting. When they went inside all was quiet. Finn pointed to the door of the bedroom, saying, "The body lies in that room sir. When I left, the mistress was also in there." At that moment Esther opened the kitchen door and came across to Finn's side. By the light of the lamp she carried, he could see that she looked as if she would faint at any moment. "Is she still in there with him?" he asked.

Nodding she said low, "Nelly and I tried to calm her but every time we opened the door, she began to scream at us, so we feared she would come at one of us so shut the door, deciding it best to leave her be until you returned."

The oldest trooper that Finn was now sure was in charge of the others confirmed it then by saying, "I'm Lieutenant Figmore. We will take care of matters now. Please go back into the kitchen and stay there until called." Barely had Finn closed the kitchen door behind them than Mona began her shrieking again, this time at the Lieutenant, shouting vile curses at him. Cora was curled in a corner by the hearth with Becky at her side, both whimpering like puppies. Nelly sat at the table, her hands fiddling in agitation on the table in front of her. Finn took Esther's hand and encouraged her to sit beside him.

Barely a minute passed before after one blood-curdling scream, such a ruckus started that Finn and Esther rushed to the door. As Finn opened it one of the younger soldiers ran to them and screamed, "Get everyone out of here now, and make sure the horses are away from the house. I fear the woman went into some sort of fit. Seems she took the blade out of her husband and after slashing the knife across her own arm, she knocked over the lamp and so set the bed alight." He then ran outside yelling for his fellows to fetch water as quickly as they could.

Finn dragged Cora up, while Esther picked up the child. With Nelly behind them they all rushed out of the kitchen. Suddenly, Esther stopped and thrust Becky at Finn shouting, "I must fetch something. Please ensure Danny Boy and the master's horse are safe."

Stunned by her statement, Finn stood for a moment with the sobbing girl in his arms until Nelly grabbed her from him and shouted, "Get the horses."

By the time Finn reached the shed, one of the troopers was leading the two horses out. Finn watched him until he was sure he had them well away from the house and when he turned back his heart turned over in his chest, for smoke was pouring from the window of the bedroom that held the mistress and dead master. His one thought was of Esther's safety, so he charged across the garden and was just about to enter the kitchen door where smoke was already billowing out, when he bumped into Esther. Dragging her by the arm he pulled her across the garden to where one of the troopers was calming the jittery horses as best he could.

The Lieutenant followed, shouting orders to the man Finn could see carrying a bucket that he must have filled up at the well. He could not make out what was said, but the man instantly dropped the bucket and followed his leader who then joined them, ordering, "We must get as far away as we can—there is little to be done for them two now." With a glance behind him, he then urged them to get further away.

From a distance they watched as the house was engulfed in flames. As luck would have it there was little wind so the flames did not reach the shed containing the two carts. Becky had gone quiet as had Cora. They and Nelly were now staring at the horror before them. Finn put an arm about Esther's shoulders admonishing, "That was a foolish thing to do, Esther. What on earth was so important that you needed to go back in there to fetch it?" Finn presumed the satchel she held over a shoulder was all she had retrieved.

With a small shake of the head, she said low, "I will explain later." She then went to stand by Danny Boy, stroking his head and offering him words of comfort. The two troopers stood whispering while their leader walked away a distance and stood staring as the house crumpled into the ashes.

Finn's mind was a jumble of thoughts. Never in his life had he thought to live through a night such as this. Although he'd guessed that the mistress was not of sound mind, he somehow could not understand what had brought her to such a crime. Not knowing the master well enough to make a true judgement on the man, he nonetheless could not conceive of Mona Franklin hating her existence so much she would commit this sin.

By the time there was little left of the cottage but smouldering remains the three troupers returned, followed by a wagon carrying a man who introduced himself as a person from the magistrate's office who was in charge of this investigation. When it became obvious that there was no body to collect and nobody to take into custody for the murder, he said, "I will go back now and make my report. Who is in charge of this household now that Mr. and Mrs. Franklin are deceased?" With a glance around, his gaze settled on Finn as he demanded, "Young fellow, you seem to be the only man here, so I take it you are the one to speak to?"

Finn stared at him in total confusion as he shook his head. "No, sir, I am just a hired worker." With a gesture towards Esther he said, "I would suggest that Esther here is the one responsible for us all."

The look the man cast over Esther could only be termed as one of derision, as he rasped, "Why, she is little more than a child. Who are these other two?" He pointed towards Nelly and Cora, who sat apart from the others, looking lost and frightened.

The Lieutenant came over then and stated, "It seems, sir, that all were merely employed by the deceased. The older woman yonder was the cook, and the younger one the housemaid. The child whimpering beside them is the daughter of the deceased and young Esther here was the child's nursemaid."

With a nod that seemed to prove his disinterest, he turned back to Finn and said, "I suggest therefore that you and the nursemaid remain here until matters are resolved. Best to keep an eye on what is left here anyway. You two women can come back with us. We will provide lodgings until suitable employment can be found for you." That was said as he pointed to Nelly and

Cora. Casting a glance at Becky he added, "The child is more of a problem. Perhaps we should also take her and try and place her in care of a responsible family until we learn who is in charge of Cecil Franklin's last testament." As if giving it a small thought he said, "No doubt there will be a relative of the deceased who will take the child under their care." Rubbing his chin as if an idea had just occurred, he added, "There is a certain female that comes to mind who might be interested in caring for the child in the meantime."

As if they were in a trance, Nelly and Cora allowed one of the troopers to lead them to the wagon. Looking back at Esther, Nelly nodded, but Cora climbed into the wagon without a backward glance. When the trooper tried to lift Becky, she began to scream and ran towards Esther where she put her arms about Esther's legs screaming that she wanted to stay with her.

Kneeling before the girl, Esther said softly, "That is impossible dearest one, for we have no food here or even a sip of milk. Go with Nelly and this kind gentleman will see that you are looked after."

Becky wiped at her runny nose and glared at the man from the magistrate's office yelling, "Don't wanna go with him. I hate him, he's a nasty man. I want to stay by you."

Rubbing her brow which was now covered in soot, Esther sighed. "I will come and see you the moment I am able. Please be a good girl and go with Nelly and Cora. They will look after you." The look she cast at Finn over the child's head clearly said that she was unsure of that happening. The pair seemed to be incapable of comprehending all that was happening.

Ordering two of the troopers to stay behind, the man nodded at Finn before climbing aboard the wagon. As it trundled off, the screams from Becky could be heard clearly above the jingle of the harness.

Lieutenant Figmore mounted and before he and the other troopers followed the wagon, he said, "I will ensure someone returns with supplies and a report of what will happen next." With a small salute, he rode off.

As luck would have it, the fence around the horse's yard had escaped the flames so Finn busied himself putting the horses in there, and the troopers Jenkins and Pike added their mounts. A kind of eerie quiet seemed to have settled over everything.

Chapter Four

Esther sat with her head on her bent knees, staring at the flames before her. Luckily the rain had stopped as dawn crept nearer. One of the troopers had managed to get the small fire going using the flint he carried. After the two men had rummaged about in the ruins of the kitchen they returned with the blackened kettle and a couple of tin mugs. Pike, who was the youngest and had the very small makings of a moustache, said, "We carry tea and usually have our billycan with us, but as we were only on a short survey looking for any runaways, we carried just the bare supplies."

He now handed her a mug of the brew, which was at least hot. "Thank you, this is lovely." Esther hoped that when someone returned with supplies, they at least carried milk and porridge and perhaps some bread and cheese.

As he walked away to join his mate who was again sorting through the rubble that had stopped smouldering, Finn sat beside her and sipped on his drink. "How do you feel?" Giving her a thoughtful glance, he rubbed at his chin. "What a mess. Can you believe the woman would do such a thing?"

"Never in my life. I knew she was desperately unhappy of course, but how she could take a blade to her husband and then take her own life is a tragedy far beyond my understanding. You have probably seen more insane people than I have."

"A few in my time." With a shrug, he stared into his mug. "Most go crazy after spending a time in solitary with little food and no light."

A thought occurred to Esther as her tummy roiled at the thought of the suffering of those folk, plus what she guessed might be hunger pangs. "I guess if they do not return later with supplies, we can always go over to the farm." She nodded in the general direction of where she knew Nellie often went to collect milk, butter, and cheese. "I expect the farmer and his wife will be wondering at the flames they must have seen rising."

As the words left her mouth, a wagon came trundling towards them. As it neared, the driver, a man that Esther had seen a few times, waved his hat as he stared at the ruins of the cottage. "What in the Lord's name happened?" he asked as he pulled the horse up and jumped down. "The master sent me across to see what was amiss."

Pike came over and put a hand up before asking the man's name and what farm he had come from. Without too many details he then explained some of the happenings of the night, leaving out the murder and suicide. "Go back and tell your master that we would be grateful if he could supply us with a few necessities like milk and bread and perhaps he might have some fresh meat. When our Lieutenant returns, he will arrange payment."

Nodding enthusiastically the man gave the ruins another quick glance, and then shook his head in Esther and Finn's direction before climbing aboard and urging his horse into a near gallop.

"Would you like me to heat some water for you, Miss? Perhaps you might like to wash the grime off you," Pike said as he sent Esther a smile. "It's good luck that the well is still in working order."

Esther returned his smile. "That would be lovely. How very thoughtful of you. I suppose I am looking as grimy as all you men are."

By the time all of them had washed some of the soot and dust from their hands and faces using a very small piece of soap that one of the troopers found during his rummaging through the remains of the kitchen, the wagon returned. Esther was drying her hands on her skirt edge, when she saw that the farmer's wife had come too, producing plates for the roast mutton, fresh baked bread, and also mugs.

"Where will you go?" she asked of Esther and Finn as they ate. "We are always in need of helpers at the farm, so you would be more than welcome to join us."

"I haven't thought that far ahead yet," Esther said. "I think I would like to go back to Hobart. We lived there for a while before my Papa took the position down here, and I enjoyed my time there." In truth, Esther had no idea what she wished to do, but her plans certainly had not included toiling long hours for a farmer and his wife.

"And where has Nelly gone?" The woman looked about as if expecting the cook to pop up from somewhere.

"Oh, she went back with the Magistrate." Esther waved her hand. She was not about to go into more details with this woman who she felt sure was in a hurry to find out all the facts so she could then spread the word to the locals.

"And Mister and Missus Franklin? Lovely lady, not that I knew her well—only met her once or twice." A glint lit her eyes as she asked this.

Esther knew not what to answer to that, so said nothing but carried on eating. Obviously sensing that she must find out all the facts at a later day the woman jumped up saying, "Well, lots to do so I'd best get back. I'll send old Briggs back for the plates and mugs."

"Thank you again for your wonderful gifts. The food was most welcome." Esther stood and waved as the wagon trundled off.

The troopers took the used dishes to wash them at the well, and then went back to searching amongst the debris of the house for a while before lying down beneath the nearby tree that remained unscathed, where they both dozed off. Finn offered his comb to Esther so that she could tidy her hair. He then gave all the horses a share of grain and ensured they had water enough for all four and then came to sit beside Esther. "Perhaps you should also try to rest for a while, it has been a trying time for certain."

"I fear I cannot. I keep reliving the sight in my head of the master lying there covered in his blood, Finn. What possessed her to kill him, I wonder?"

"That we will never know, Esther. Tell me, do you really intend to go to Hobart once this is all sorted out?"

Esther shrugged as she looked across the surrounding paddocks. "I will wait and see. I feel as if I am in a bad dream. One of those where you wander about in search of something but are not sure what. A certainty is that I do not wish to stay anywhere around here. I keep thinking of Becky and wondering how the child is faring."

"We will learn once the Magistrate makes his decision." Finn lay back, hands beneath his head. After a short time, Esther realised by his steady breathing that he had gone to sleep. Nibbling on her lower lip she watched his chest as it rose and fell steadily. What if he decided that now he could make his own way and had no desire to stay with her—that thought made her feel quite sad. In a short time, he had come to mean a lot to her and she was unsure just why. Perhaps it had something to do with her being lonely, and him coming along to fill a vast gap that had appeared in her life after losing her parents.

The sun was high in the sky when she awoke suddenly, realising that she had snuggled into Finn's side like a lost puppy. With a start she sat up and rubbed at her eyes. The troopers were sitting a short distance away, smoking on their clay pipes and chatting quietly. The jangle of harness warned of an approaching vehicle so she shook Finn's shoulder, saying, "I think they have returned."

He sat up, stretching his arms above his head as he looked towards what Esther now realised was not one but two carriages coming towards them. Jenkins and Pike jumped to their feet and came across to stand near Esther and Finn as they all watched the vehicles and the Lieutenant and one other trooper draw near.

Lieutenant Figmore dismounted and handed over his reins to Pike, while the carriages halted a small distance away. Puzzled, Esther whispered to Finn, "Why have they brought two carriages? We certainly do not need to be taken anywhere. I have my own gig and horse." As the words left her mouth, a woman descended from the rear carriage, then turned to offer help to a child. "Goodness, she has brought Becky back," Esther exclaimed as the girl ran full pelt towards them.

Throwing her arms about Esther, Becky squealed, "I have a new home—with her." She jabbed a finger in the woman's direction. "Guess what? I have an almost brother. Eric's only a baby, well he is five, but as I am bigger than he is I can tell him what to do."

Lost for words, Esther stared at the woman as she came towards her and Finn, an arm extended. "Good day to you. I presume you are the Esther who Becky talks non-stop about." Her grip was firm as she took Esther's hand in her gloved one, before leaning in close to mutter, "The poor child seems to have forgotten the events that occurred here, which is fortunate." Releasing her grip, she looked at the ruins of the house in silence, before saying, "Oh my goodness, it must all have been awful for you. Poor Cecil, my brother did not deserve such an end. I never did take to the foolish woman he was determined to make his wife. Our poor Papa was driven into an early grave over the match that proved a failure. The only good thing that came out of it is the child." This last was said in almost a whisper.

Esther was still reeling at the realisation that this person was the master's sister and not his mistress. How wrong they had been. By the look of the clothes she wore, she was not exactly of the gentry but most definitely was not a pauper who depended on her brother for her existence. "Yes, I am Esther, and this is Finn who also worked for Mr. and Mrs. Franklin." She gestured to Finn who currently was bending to listen to Becky's chatter. "I am so glad that you were able to care for Becky. I was worried that she might end up in the orphanage. How fortunate for her that you are a relative."

The woman drew out a kerchief from the small purse she carried and wiped at a small tear that had fallen down her cheek. No raving beauty she had a pleasant face, with no sign that she was related to Mr. Franklin. Although she appeared to be likely in her mid-thirties, light hair that was almost silver peeped from beneath her bonnet. Sniffing back more tears, she nodded as she said, "Yes, I am Priscilla Clements. My dear husband was killed unfortunately soon after we arrived here at the garrison, and so my brother convinced me it would be best to stay here where he was nearby." Glancing again at the ruined cottage she asked, "What do you intend doing now that there is no reason to stay here? I surmise you will be in need of fresh employment."

Esther nodded as she looked at Finn who stood a few paces away. He seemed to have a question in his eyes. No need to tell this woman that she could quite easily now go wherever she wished as her Papa had ensured that she would not be without means, she knew her decision depended on what Finn decided. Foolish of her she knew, but if he now went his own way, she would be downhearted—or perhaps even heartbroken.

"I have decided to go back to Hobart now that there is no reason for me to stay in this damned part of the country, and perhaps you would consider travelling with me. I know that you have been teaching Becky her lessons as surprisingly the child is well versed in some subjects. She is certainly more intelligent than my son who until now has been looked after by a nanny."

Before Esther could respond, the stranger who had been in the other carriage came across and introduced himself as the Magistrate who had been charged with overseeing this whole business. "I have studied the ruins and heard the case from the Lieutenant here." With a small gesture at the trooper, he said, "I suppose there is nothing left here for you and therefore you are free to go. There seems to be little doubt over exactly what took place here." As if to turn away, he came back and added, "I could not help but overhear what Madam Clements said, and in my honest opinion you would be foolish not to accept her offer. As chief benefactor of Mr. Franklin's estate, whatever still remains intact here is now her property." With a small wave towards Finn, he said, "You, young fellow, is there anything of value in the building yonder?" That was said with a gesture towards the shed.

Rubbing his ear, Finn said, "The master's small wagon is in there plus the one that belongs to Miss Blythe here. There are some tools that may be of value and horse fodder and hay." With a nod towards the small paddock where all the horses were now at the fence as if interested in the proceedings, he added, "The larger bay is also the property of the master."

"Right, in that case if you can drive Mr. Franklin's vehicle, I would suggest that whatever your decision for now you should follow the good lady here to her home. Pack the wagon with whatever she decides to keep." Without further ado, he turned to beckon the lieutenant to his side, gave him a few muttered orders before walking to his carriage.

As it trundled away, Esther beckoned to Finn before walking off a few paces. "I think I will take his advice, Finn, and go with Madam Clements. You are free to go wherever you choose now, so perhaps you are not interested in accompanying me." Inwardly she held her breath as she looked at him.

Rubbing at his chin while he seemed to think it over, he then said, "Well, to be honest, I wouldn't mind going to Hobart. I do not have a heap of choices, do I? My circumstances remain the same as when you kindly brought me here, as I have not received any kind of wage, have I?" That last was said with a small chuckle.

Although slightly disappointed that he had not mentioned that he in some small way did not wish to be parted from her, Esther was nonetheless pleased at his decision. Together they went over to tell their new employer they had decided to take up her offer.

Mrs. Clements' driver, a likeable man called Will, offered his help, so by the time her carriage and the two carts had been readied and loaded with as much as could be carried, it was late afternoon. The troopers were going to camp here for another night so they farewelled them and set off. Becky insisted on riding alongside Esther, and chatted as if she had no memory of the disaster that had happened. Esther followed Mrs. Clements carriage and Finn trailed her. The short journey bypassed the prison, a building that had an eerie quiet about it, and Esther realised they were heading north. It seemed odd to her that Madam Clements had chosen to stay down here after her husband's demise, but could be that Mr. Franklin was her only close relative in this country.

"It's a nice house," Becky said when Esther pulled Danny up behind the carriage that stopped before a cottage not much different to the one just left behind. Esther wondered just where they would all fit in, plus what they carried.

Will climbed down and came over to stand beside Esther's cart. "Madam says it might be best to not unload the vehicles tonight, as it will soon be dark. Follow me around the back and you can put the horses in the small field there where they will be safe. There is not room in the stable unfortunately, but you can put your carts in the small shelter yonder. It is open to the weather but at least there is some cover in case it rains overnight." He climbed aboard and drove the carriage towards this building.

Before their new employer entered the house, she gave orders for them to follow her inside once the animals were settled. "Come Becky, it is time you were in your bed." She lifted the girl down from the carriage amid her protests, just as a young girl came running out of the cottage. "Ruby, take the girl. Is Eric already settled?" she asked of her.

"Yes, ma'am." Esther guessed that this Ruby was the nanny, although she looked barely old enough to look after herself let alone a child.

Esther and Finn were about to lead their horses to the small field when loud shouts came from the stable that Will had entered. "Here, take him, and I'll see what the problem is," Finn said as he handed the leading reins to her before running towards the barn. Esther heard him call, "You all right, Will?" as he entered. Then she gasped as a menacing shape loomed from the shadows, lunging at Finn. "What in hell's name?" he yelled as she saw him aim at a large man's head.

His assailant seemed to be a giant, towering over Finn who was by no means short of stature. After a few grunts and a short tussle Finn had the man pinned to the ground face down. Still grunting words not fit for the ears of a decent woman, the man fought some more but when Will, holding at his jaw which had obviously been punched, came to his aid and knelt on the giant's legs, his grunts subsided. Esther clearly heard him call Finn by name.

"Do you know this person?" she asked as she came closer, still leading the two horses.

"That I do. This bloke is the one that sent me off to hospital with a busted shoulder." With a thump at the back of the man's head, Finn added, "He goes by the name of Bear. Nasty piece of work if ever there was one. Not so clever now, are you?" That was followed by another smart whack on the head of the giant who had now gone quiet.

"I'll put the horses away and fetch some rope to secure him with. Do you think he has escaped from the prison?"

"Well, Bear, is that what you were doing when we nabbed you?" Finn gave the man another swift slap on the shoulder.

"Can't blame a bloke for trying, can you?" the man named Bear mumbled.

Esther led the horses into the small field and secured the gate once she had let them free. "There's some sturdy rope just inside the stable yonder," Will pointed to the small structure. Just as the words left his mouth two riders came into view. As they neared, Esther could see that they were troopers. "Well, I'll be blowed, looks like it isn't your lucky day, is it Bear, my lad. Likely on the lookout for the likes of you, I'd say." Will waved and called out to them.

In no time at all, the troopers, who had indeed been on the lookout for the escapee had him trussed up and were headed back to the prison, one of them dragging the protesting Bear alongside his horse. "I'll get yer for this, Irish Finn," he threatened loudly, still swearing curses at Finn until they were out of hearing.

"That was a pretty good job you did, Finn old fellow," Will said as he patted Finn's shoulder. "Ever thought of trying your hand at a bit of fist fighting?" He glanced about before adding in a softer voice, "I've heard some codgers make a tidy sum in the ring."

Finn laughed as he shook his head. "Haven't had a lot of time for such to be honest, but a man has to be handy with his fists where I've been for the past ten years."

"Come on, let's get your horses fed and get everything under cover." As Will patted Finn's shoulder again the girl Ruby came from the house at a run.

"The missus said there is food waiting for you. Best get inside, quick smart. Cook ain't in the best of moods, having extra mouths to feed." Just as quickly she scurried back inside.

"It's not much, but the best I could do at such short notice," the cook, who told them she went by the name of Alma said as she waved them to the table in the kitchen.

Their new mistress Mrs. Clements, sat at the end of the table that barely had enough room for them all. She had the only chair and Finn and Esther sat very close to each other on one of the benches at each side with Becky aside Esther. Once she had placed dishes in the centre of the table, Alma, along with Will and Ruby settled opposite them. "We have never needed a lot of room," Mrs. Clements said once they were seated. "Let us eat and then perhaps we should all get some rest. I suggest that we begin our travels on the morrow."

"This is delicious, Alma," Esther said as she helped herself to cold meats and various vegetables.

"Ain't much," the cook mumbled as she, too, tucked into the food. "There won't be anything to follow, for I didn't have time."

Later, Esther yawned as she climbed into the narrow bed beside Becky who was already sound asleep. The boy Eric apparently slept on a cot in his Mama's room. Esther wondered how Finn fared as he had gone off with Will to bed down in the stable. Pulling the nightgown Mrs. Clements had given her over her knees, Esther barely had time to contemplate what the new day would bring before sleep claimed her.

Chapter Five

Finn stretched and sat up. Dawn had not quite arrived as he pulled on his shirt and breeches. Will still snored on his bed of straw. Before falling asleep Finn had gone over the extraordinary events of the past days. He had seen some rare sights and met some strange buggers over his lifetime of struggle and imprisonment but his now dead employers just about were at the top of the list of odd ones. And now it seems he and Esther were in the employ of another strange one. Still unable to quite come to terms with all the facts, he wondered just why a woman who was obviously not short of means should choose to stay in this neck of the woods simply because of a wish to be near her brother. A lover he could perhaps understand.

Then again, what did he know of love and its peculiarities. Joe Spence, his pit mate when logging, had also shared their meagre bed space when locked up. Being of what he called a poetic bent, his stories of his dead wife who he often pined over, were the nearest Finn had ever come to hearing or thinking on what Spence called this love business. The death of his wife while giving birth had just about sent poor old Spence to hell, and likely sent him off on the life of crime that got him locked up.

Finn's one venture into something that might border on what people called love was with a street woman who took a fancy on him. It happened just before his capture. At fifteen he of course had listened to the older boys bragging on what they called their conquests, and it was their jibes that egged him on to take the woman's offer. Tall for his age so he was told, she said after the fumbling effort on his part that she liked young boys, for they didn't stink quite as much as her usual customers. The whole shenanigans gave him something to brag about to the younger lads for a long time. Anyway, she let him off when he offered to steal a gift for her, as at the time he had not a farthing to his name.

As he portioned out grain and hay for the horses, his thoughts went to Esther, a young woman who had now seen tragedy of the worst kind. Unlike the street floosy, Esther always smelled nice, and her lovely scent seemed to linger after she moved away. For some reason he had an urge to please his rescuer as he'd pleased nobody before. Hopefully she was strong enough to weather this new episode in her life. What would it be like, he wondered, to lay with her, to feel the joy Spence had told him about that came with not only sharing your life with another, but sharing those special feelings that he called proper love. Along with that thought came the next, which was just what choice did he really have but to now journey to Hobart with them all and take whatever life was about to throw his way next.

As he finished feeding the animals, Will joined him, stretching and yawning. "If you've finished that, Finn, we'll have a quick sluice at the well and see what Alma has cooked up for us. Not a bad cook that woman," he said on a chuckle.

Alma was indeed a good cook, Finn thought, as he tucked into the pork rashers, eggs and mushrooms along with freshly baked bread that she placed before them on the table. "Missus says she would like to start our journey as soon as you men have everything packed. No sense in staying here where we all barely have room to lay our heads at night," she said. "I'll get one of you to help me stow the rations once I have done some more preparing." Using the hem of her apron to wipe at her furrowed brow she added, "Been at it most of the night I have, baking and boiling just so there's plenty to eat along the way."

Esther came into the kitchen looking refreshed and pretty in a garment Finn guessed had been provided by their new missus. Her beautiful hair was fashioned into what he thought they called a braid that hung over one shoulder. She smiled at him before sitting down alongside Becky who gabbled on in her obvious excitement about the news that they would be travelling as soon as all was packed and ready. "The Mistress has a few of her husband's garments that she thinks will fit you, Finn," Esther said. "She said for you to go along the passage there to the room at the end and she will tell you what you can take and also what to put in the trunks. It seems the furniture belongs here in the cottage, so nothing of any size will be going with her."

Acknowledging her with a nod, Finn had a feeling that his stupid face had gone quite red. It certainly felt hot. Later, with his new possessions bundled and packed in the old master's cart along with other packages, he felt quite well turned out in a new shirt and even boots that fortunately had fit him well. It took him and Will quite some time to load everything, including the horse's fodder and grain, onto the missus's carriage, plus the two carts, so by the time everyone was ready to make a start on their journey the sun was already well up in the sky.

Alma and Ruby rode along with their mistress and the boy Eric, while Becky insisted on being alongside Esther. They made one stop at a nearby farmhouse to notify the farmer that they had left the cottage, which it seemed was his property. Alma also picked up more eggs and other necessities that they would need on their arrival.

For a while the road took them alongside the railway line that the government had taken great pride in installing when announcing it was the first in Van Diemen's Land. Propelled along by poor buggers from the prison, the carriage moved no faster than their carts and for a while they endured the insults thrown their way by the cons. The road then ran along the clifftop with the sea on their left. The ocean held no attraction for Finn after the voyage from hell he and the other lads transported alongside him had to endure. One lad not much older than ten, died during a dreadful stormy night where for hours they were tormented by the rocking and heaving of the ship. So weakened by sickness he had been flung out of his bunk. There was little they could do to assist him so the lad had lain where he fell until the storm subsided on the morrow.

Finn's insides did a somersault when their small cavalcade reached Eaglehawk Neck and they were halted by the dreaded guards and their vicious dogs. He touched his pocket that held the paper proving he was a free man, but after having a few words with Priscilla Clements the men waved them on their way. Nevertheless, one of the guards with nasty eyes stared hard at Finn as he trundled past. Finn breathed a sigh of relief, feeling ensured that he really was a free man now, and would never set foot in this neck of the woods again.

After travelling across country for a while, Will pulled off the road and stopped where a few trees gave shade. They had seen no other travelers along the way. There was little tasty grass for the horses to pick at after a particularly hot summer, so Finn and Will gave each a handful of hay to munch on. Alma brought out a basket that contained meat slices, cheese and bread and for a while they all sat in silence while eating. Eric and Becky began to chant some childish rhyme as they ran around.

"How are you faring?" Finn asked Esther as she sat with eyes closed, looking somewhat weary.

The smile she sent him was slightly askew. "I cannot lie, Finn, but I shall be glad when I can set myself down without feeling that the world is all topsy turvy." Leaning closer, she said low, "I cannot believe how our lives have changed so, and all within a short time."

"That's a fact." With a nod towards where their new employer sat, also looking tired, he added, "I have a feeling that Mrs. Clements will perhaps be a more suitable missus." Pausing while he pondered on how to ask his next question, he dared ask, "Could you not perhaps consider seeking new employment when we reach Hobart Town?"

Before answering, she watched the children for a while, then said, "Because this tragedy has followed on so swiftly from the past where I lost my dear parents, I have no real desire to take on new ventures."

They said no more and soon were on their way again. It seemed as if they had covered many miles and dusk was falling when they reached an inn of sorts. The missus thought rightly that it was best if Will and Finn slept in the carriage so that they could ensure the safety of their belongings and also the horses who were in a small yard alongside three other horses belonging to travelers.

The sun was just appearing above the horizon as they set off again. Earlier Will told Finn that he doubted they would make Hobart Town this day, but it depended on the weather and how the horses held up. As he and the other convicts were transported down from New South Wales by ship, Finn had no idea of the distance as they were all kept below decks the entire time, where all they had to think about was what the future now held for them. He'd met Spence on that journey, and was fortunate that the Scot had taken a liking to him.

Will proved right, for soon after passing over a bridge that he told Finn later was the first of its kind built in these parts, they stopped at another inn. Everyone was weary after the days travelling, so Finn barely had time to pass more than a few moments with Esther before they settled down for the night—he and Will bedding down in the carriage again. At the crack of dawn, they were off on what Will said was the final leg of the journey. Finn admitted to himself that he was rather enjoying the freedom this journey had offered him. The new missus had kept herself aloof while they travelled, making him wonder what life would be like living in her home. So far, she had made no mention of her intentions, in fact was similar to her brother in that she did not talk a lot. Perhaps it was more because they were all her staff and that was how she treated those who worked for her. Finn thought how lonely that existence was.

Once they crossed over the causeway into the city, Will pulled up and came over to stand beside Esther's cart. "You are to stay here while the missus visits her agent. It seems that she sent a telegraph to her agent arranging for a house to be readied for her." With a nod towards Finn, he went back and climbed aboard.

Finn climbed down and stood beside Esther's cart, offering her a hand. "We may as well stretch our legs a bit while we wait. Not sure about you, but I feel as if I am sorely in need of a walk." He wasn't about to mention such to her but his rear end felt as if it had been sitting in the same position for ever.

She took his hand and allowed him to help her down. Becky also waited on him to lift her down. "Mrs. Clements mentioned last night before we slept that she felt sure her agent would find her something most suitable to rent until she can arrange to see what is on offer for sale," Esther said as she straightened her skirts. Leaning closer so that Becky could not hear, she added softly, "I have a feeling our new employer is by no means a poor woman, for apart from Becky she is the only beneficiary of her brother's estate."

Finn had surmised as much. The woman, although very pleasant, had an air about her that most members of the gentry possessed. A fact that made him wonder again just why she had chosen to stay out miles from society simply to be near her brother. But what did he know of family loyalty? The gang he lived with in London were the closest he had ever come to having a family of sorts to call his own. "Do you know the city very well?" he asked, unsure of Esther's past, except for knowing she and her parents moved to Port Arthur where her Pa took on his work as a doctor.

"Not really. I was just a child of about four years of age when we arrived at the colony in New South Wales, and had reached about seventeen when Papa was asked to come down here." With a deep sigh, she added, "Perhaps they would still be alive had we stayed on up there."

Finn said nothing to that. It was clear that she had not reached a stage of fully accepting that they were gone. His own history had taught him that nothing is permanent in this life—and perhaps that knowledge had hardened him. Whether that was good or not was beyond his understanding.

The road was quite busy and many vehicles trundled by in both directions. Most drivers eyed them with a touch of interest or suspicion. The afternoon was growing cooler as the sun began to go down. When Will came back, he pulled his horse to a stop, and did not climb down but signaled for them to follow him. It did not take long for them to reach what was by no means a grand house, but certainly one that was larger than the cottage they left.

As they had passed along the streets, Finn looked about with interest. There was an air of prosperity about—not that he could see much but the fences fronting some of the larger houses that held two floors. But he recalled how London often reeked of a million stenches. There had been no time to look about after arriving on the ship, for they were all instantly trundled off to the prison that he never left until they sailed down the coast to Van Diemen's Land.

After ordering Will and Finn to get about it and unload the food first, Alma bustled inside after her mistress and Ruby who had a sleeping Eric over one shoulder. There was little time for them to pass more than a word or two with each other before everyone retired to their beds. The stables at the back of the large garden behind the house contained stalls for four horses, plus a separate space for the carriage and carts. By the time Finn lay down and pulled a blanket over himself on a bed of straw in the empty stall beside Will, he was more tired than when logging. Barely having a thought about how lucky he was, he was asleep.

A cock crowed somewhere close by, rousing Finn. A streak of pale light lit the stables as he pulled on his new shirt and breeches, feeling quite pleased with the new turn of events. For the first time in his life, he had a selection of clothes to pull on. He visited the privy beside the stables, and then sloshed water over his hands and face at the pump. Will stirred as Finn was feeding the horses. Soon the two of them entered the kitchen where Alma was already busily working at the stove. "If you would be so good as to fetch some water before you eat, I'd appreciate it," she said to Finn with a nod.

He was just tucking in to eggs, bacon and bread fried in bacon fat, when Esther came into the kitchen followed by the two children. The smile she sent Finn's way was warmer than the morning sun streaming in through the one window, sending a glow of heat right to his heart. "The mistress will take breakfast in her room," she informed Alma before sitting opposite Finn. "She is unsure how long it will take the agent to find a suitable house for her so it seems we may stay here for a time—or perhaps a matter of days."

As it happened just a week or so later, they were on the move again. The days were growing shorter, showing signs of autumn as they trundled again through the streets. Their route took them through an area that Will had explained was populated by the poorer folk. "It is said that the slum area along the wharf is well known for drunkenness and revelry, and such pastimes as cock fighting are held. Recall I mentioned that you could earn a tidy sum with your fists, lad? Well, that's where it is most likely to happen."

Finn had not thought any more on that subject, being too occupied with the day-today tasks required of him that kept him busy from sun up until dusk. Esther had been occupied with the children as well as teaching them their sums and letters. He hoped that once they were settled again, they would be able to spend more time together. It seemed that they had rarely had time to pass more than a few words with each other since their journey began. Although not harsh, Mrs. Clements certainly ensured that her staff, although small, did not shirk in their duties. After his treatment through the years at the hands of some guards, he found her kind, and in thinking about it, perhaps shy or unused to ordering her servants about.

Their small cavalcade drew some attention as they headed past open land to their right that Will had told Finn was parkland set aside for the enjoyment of the general public. The houses seemed to be set more apart with larger areas surrounding them. When they followed the carriage as Will drove through a pair of large ornate gates, the house loomed before them. Finn had not expected such a fine residence, although he had no doubt of their mistress's wealth by now. It compared in size to the one in London with two floors that he was taken to as a child by the English woman.

The next day, Esther approached Finn as he was brushing Danny Boy beside the stables where there was plenty of room for four horses as well as all their vehicles. With a smile his way, she sat herself down on the bench against the wall. "He's looking well," she said, nodding her horse's way. "How are you settling in, Finn? It has been quite a journey, hasn't it? What with one thing and another, we have barely had time to dally since meeting our new mistress."

Finn sat beside her and stretched his legs before him. "To be honest, Esther, I keep pinching myself when I wonder how this all came about. If not for you rescuing me, I wonder where I would be now." Glancing towards the brick-built house he added, "I certainly wouldn't be in such a position as I am now."

"I have a feeling that you would do well whatever circumstances you found yourself in." He wasn't as sure of that as she seemed to be. Rising she went to pat her horse's soft nose. "I have an errand to make, and Mrs. Clements agreed that it would be best if you accompanied me—if you agree of course."

Intrigued, he stared at her. Of course, there was no doubt in his mind by now that he would go anywhere with this young woman or do anything within his power to help her. "When do you wish to go?"

"Ruby is capable of watching over the children for a while, so perhaps we could go now. I need to visit the bank, which is in

Macquarie Street, so we do not have to go far. Perhaps we could walk as it is a fine day."

Even more interested now, he rose. "I will put Danny back in his stall and then I am ready to go."

"Just give me a moment or two to fetch my bonnet and jacket."

As she walked back to the house, Finn went across to the pump and washed his hands and face, then went into the small shack alongside the stable where he and Will now slept, brushed his hair and because it now reached below his shoulders, he tied it back with a piece of string. Pulling his jacket on, he went outside just as Esther came from the house. He noted that beneath her arm she carried the small satchel of importance that was the only thing she had thought to rescue from the burning cottage.

"I expect you are wondering just why I am going to the bank," she said as they strolled along. A few carts and carriages trundled past.

Finn had wondered, but would not make comment. "Not at all," he said. In fact, his life had taken so many unexpected turns since meeting this incredible woman he had come to accept everything as it came along.

Patting the satchel across her shoulder, she said, "On the day that my Papa handed this to me, to my utter surprise he said that he had ensured that in the event of anything happening to him or my dear Mama, I would never have cause to want for the necessities of life." With a huge sigh, she continued, "Of course, he or I would never have dreamed that a short time later the worst possible thing befell them."

Finn had an almost irresistible urge to take her in his arms and offer comfort. For a brief moment he wondered how she would react if he did such a thing. Apart from all the assistance she had given him, she had shown no interest in furthering their relationship into anything more than friendship. "If that is the case, then why did you choose to go into the home of the Franklin's?" he asked instead.

"As I explained when we first met, I was in search of finding a place for myself in society, a place—perhaps a haven, where I would be part of a family." Shrugging, she said, "Sadly that did not end well, did it?" They strolled in silence for a while before she gave him a look he didn't understand, then said, "At least it brought us into each other's lives, Finn. I hope you consider that a benefit."

"Oh, believe me, I do." Earnestly he hurried to add, "If you had not assisted me, I dread to think where my wanderings would have taken me. Perhaps I would have ended up with a scoundrel like that Bear fellow or a band of bushrangers."

She stopped walking and for a moment Finn simply stared at her, until she said, "We have reached my destination. Would you come inside with me, Finn? I fear I will likely be treated as the silly young woman that I am. I think perhaps I will need someone to give me the confidence required to face a man of business."

"You most certainly are not as silly as you profess, but to be honest, I have never been inside such a place as a bank, so I will willingly accompany you, if only to see what happens in such an establishment. I met a couple of coves in prison who had attempted to rob one like this up in Sydney Town." With a jerk of the head towards the door of the bank, he added. "It seems the gentry leave their loot here and this is kept in a safe. These silly buggers had got themselves a stick of dynamite or two with the intention of blowing the thing to smithereens. All they did was nearly get themselves blown sky high before being nabbed and earning themselves a nice long stay in the penitentiary."

Finn had often wondered what it would be like to have money jangling in his pocket, but after hearing their sorry tale he doubted he would ever go to such lengths to get it. Only last night Will had once again mentioned the place where Finn could perhaps earn himself some of these pounds by using his fists, and his interest was indeed roused.

He pushed open the door, and gestured for her to go before him. Staring about at the drab room, he felt slightly disappointed. He'd half expected to see this thing called a safe with perhaps a guard sitting in front of it to protect the earnings of the rich folk. But there was just a man who looked to be not much older than Finn himself sitting behind a huge desk. This man looked straight at Finn as he said, "Good afternoon, Sir, Madam, what can I do this fine afternoon to assist you?"

With a hand on her arm, he pushed Esther before him.

Chapter Six

As they left the building, Esther felt quite faint with dizziness. She had suspected that her parents were most definitely not poor, but to now know that she was what in her estimation was a rich woman was something that would take getting used to. Finn had not spoken to her since they left the manager of the bank's office, and she had a feeling that he was just as stunned as she. To know that had she wanted to, she could purchase a grand house similar to that owned by Priscilla Clements was hard to believe.

Of course, she had some idea that her Grandmama had left her Mama with a substantial legacy when she departed this world. Added to that her dear Papa's Grandparent had also not been without means. She recollected that once she heard her parents discussing the circumstances that had brought them to this land on the other side of the world, and had a sense that there had been some animosity between them and Grandpapa. Her Mama refused to enlighten her to the reason they were not on good terms with their parents, so Esther was left to wonder at the circumstances that sent them on an epic voyage with their four-year-old daughter.

"Shall we be going back now?" Finn asked, interrupting her jumbled thoughts.

"Um, no, it is so nice to be away from the children for a while, so perhaps we could dally."

"As you wish." Esther was not certain but sensed a slight wariness in him that hadn't been there before. She began to walk slowly with him at her side.

They had gone quite a way in silence before he asked, "What do you intend to do now? Perhaps you are thinking of leaving Mrs. Clements' home and heading off to make a life on you own?" Unsure of it, she thought perhaps he sounded despondent, but perhaps that was simply her imagination.

"I have no intentions of going elsewhere—at least not in the foreseeable future, Finn. And where would I go?" A sudden thought came to mind and she blurted, "Have you ever yearned to return to your homeland?"

"Goodness, no, for I have no good memories, except those few spent with my fellow gang members. I have no reason to go back to Ireland, for I have no memories of that place at all. Why do you ask?" He seemed shaken by her question. "You do not have it in mind to go back to England, do you?"

"The thought only just occurred to me for I know that I have close relatives back there, and also have lots of unanswered questions as to why my parents left there under unhappy circumstances. Perhaps if they had lived, one day they might have seen fit to explain those circumstances to me." Esther sighed. "Do you not sometimes yearn to return to Ireland where you were born— and to perhaps track down the family of the woman who bore you?"

"The thought never occurred to me, as I always knew that it was an impossibility. I was told later that the gypsy woman who took me as her own vowed that my Ma had died, but perhaps she lied. And if there were family, then surely they would have taken me in as a baby, instead of letting some stranger take me away."

"But your Mama is the one who named you, I presume."

With a shake of the head, he said, "Truth is I picked my name, for I did not ever fancy the posh name the English woman gave to me. Why would I wish to go by the name of

Gilbert?" His disgust was plain to see. "I was mostly called Boy by the family anyway."

Esther stared at him in surprise. "How extraordinary. So why did you set on the name of Finn? It is a good name by the way."

"Well, as it happened, one of the boys I lived with in London stole a book at the market one day, and it was penned by an Irishman who had a love it seemed for tall tales that he called legends." A grin split his face. "This Finn MacCool fellow led a band of warriors who were known for their bravery. They took an oath for the king to defend Ireland from attack by outsiders. It seemed he had hair of the same shade as mine—very light so it said."

What an interesting, if strange, life he had spent—so different to hers in every way. Esther could not conceive of a life where you knew not for sure where your parents came from. They walked on without speaking until they were almost back at the house, then he said, "I have no desire to go on a sailing ship again anyway, so a voyage, if by chance I could ever afford to pay the cost, is not something I would even think about."

"I was just a child when my parents decided to make the journey and do not recall either my Mama or Papa complaining of sickness, so we must have been lucky and had fair weather." Esther now wondered just why she had even mentioned a voyage—perhaps the thought of becoming a woman of means had blurred her judgement.

Later, after the children had been put into their beds, Esther sat in the small parlour alongside Mrs. Clements. Finn and Will had gone to care for the horses, and as usual Alma and Ruby were in the kitchen. Looking up from the small dress she was mending, Esther chewed on her lip as she contemplated bringing up the subject of her new state of wealth. Her employer never conversed much and Esther was never quite sure if it was due to her supposed station in life, or perhaps that she was just not the talkative type.

The woman saved Esther saying what was on her mind by asking, "Was your visit to the bank satisfactory, my dear?"

"Oh yes, ma'am, in fact more so than satisfactory." Putting the garment aside she said, "As a matter of fact I wished to ask you a question regarding wealth and position."

Mrs. Clements seemed surprised at that, and placing the embroidery she was working on aside, she asked, "Am I to presume that you found yourself in a favorable position where your inheritance is concerned?"

"Yes, it is. I knew my parents were by no means poor, having been left inheritances themselves but I have to say I had no idea that I would be in the position of trying to decide what to do next."

"Do I take that to mean that you wish to leave my house? I honestly have never considered myself your employer because of the unusual circumstances that brought us together, but would be sad to see us part company."

That was the most Priscilla Clements had said on the subject of their odd meeting. Esther guessed that was perhaps because of the disastrous events that changed all their lives—and no doubt the dear lady was still grieving. Esther sighed. "Well, more than anything, I wished to ask your advice. Most young women of my age have a parent or relative to guide them, but as I have neither I look to you for assistance in the matter of wealth."

Mrs. Clements' brows rose at that. Reaching across the small space, she patted Esther's hand. "I was in a similar position, my dear girl. That is why I looked to my brother as he was my closest relative and my strength. I doubtless would never have even left my homeland to come to this place that I do not especially like, if not for my husband." Looking at the wall over Esther's shoulder, she went on, "He was a military man and therefore had to merely follow orders. And then when he was killed so soon after our arrival, I had nowhere else to turn but to dear Cecil, poor man." For a moment she seemed to dwell in the past before saying, "I was in similar circumstances as you as far as my newly gained wealth. Back home, I was not allowed to discuss such things as money in my parent's house, so I too was in a quandary." She picked up her embroidery and for a few moments Esther thought perhaps she had no more to say but she then surprised Esther by asking, "Has marriage entered your mind?"

"Goodness no. I have not had a chance to even contemplate the idea—and who would I marry?"

"What of Finn? He seems a likeable young chap, and the pair of you seem to get on well together. In my estimation, a woman of your age would be wise to have a man at her side that she can trust—especially where newly acquired wealth is concerned." She let out a deep sigh. "It is a man's world I am afraid, and we must simply follow wherever they lead."

Esther had never disclosed how she and Finn met, and as far as she guessed, their mistress had no idea that he was so recently a prisoner of the Government. She never intended to trail behind any man. Her Mama had stressed that she should always follow her heart and her own dreams. As far as Finn went, she admitted to herself that often at night she wondered just what it would be like to have him beside her in her bed, but as far as she could estimate he had no romantic thoughts about her. Earlier this evening, he mentioned that he was going to the area near the docks where Will had suggested Finn might win a cash prize by fighting. In her heart, she knew that was not the sort of future she planned—to live with a man who used his fists in a bid to earn money. She had envisaged a life with perhaps a doctor like her Papa or someone with a similar profession.   How she yearned for her Mama's guidance in such matters.

As if reading her thoughts, Mrs. Clements went on, "In polite society Esther, in a lot of cases, romance does not enter into the negotiations where marriage is concerned. It is usually the woman's dowry that encourages a man to seek her out as a bride."

Esther wondered if perhaps that had been the case with her, but was not about to ask such an impertinent question. "Because I was very young when I came here, I know little of how weddings were arranged back home. My Mama told me that she married Papa because they shared so many interests, and I am sure they shared a deep love for each other. I do know that there was some sort of disagreement with their parents, but I have no idea if that was because of her choice of husband."

Later, as Esther lay in her comfortable bed, her mind was still whirling with what the mistress had said. Through no fault of his own, Finn had no real schooling as far as she could discern. Apart from the few years when he lived with the English family in London, his life lessons had been picked up from the streets and from other boys sharing those streets. Surprisingly he had good manners, and as far as she could discern was kind, especially with the children and the horses, and she had no reason to think otherwise.

Their relationship had been so unusual from the start—and she wondered how it might have been had they met in other circumstances. For all she knew he could be a liar and a cheat and concealing his true side from her. No man in his right frame of mind who had been a convict would turn his back on the easy life she had thrown his way. These thoughts made her feel ill-spirited. So far, her life had afforded her no contact with any other men who would make suitable husbands. Other than military men, or fellow medical men like her father, she had no man to hold up beside Finn as being a suitable choice for a husband anyway.

With a sigh and a huff, she turned over and tried to sleep. A noise woke her and she sat up. The candle had burned low, but through the small gap in the heavy curtains, she could see that it was still dark outside.

Throwing the coverlet aside she went over to the window where she could make out the stables where two figures stood outside. For a moment fear took hold and she imagined it might be thieves about to steal the horses, but then the cloud moved to display the moon and she could clearly see Finn and Will. Will held his pipe in his hand and the pair of them seemed to be deep in discussion, before Finn's laugh echoed through the trees.

Going back to sit on the side of her bed, Esther rubbed at her eyes. She liked Will, for he seemed a hard worker and got on amicably with everyone, but now that she thought about it, she knew that it had been his suggestion that Finn could use his fists to earn big money. What, she wondered, did the pair of them consider large sums of money? Since settling into the house, their employer had kindly informed Esther and Finn that she had discussed the matter with her adviser—whoever that was—and thus she would be ensuring the two of them were given a monthly stipend. That news had pleased Finn no end and he admitted it would be the first time he had ever held money in his pocket.

In actual fact, until Esther's visit to the bank, she had never known what it was to carry cash either. There had been no cause to do so before or during her position with Mona and Cecil Franklin. While her Papa was alive, everything she needed had been provided by her doting parents. A headache began to form as she lay back. When the children came running into the room, Esther awoke to see sunshine streaming through the window.

Since arriving here, most of the chores related to the children had fallen on Esther while Ruby had been occupied with taking care of the dusting and cleaning of the house. The previous owners of the property had returned to England, therefore they left behind the furnishings. Ruby seemed quite content to do all these chores and admitted to Esther that she was not overly fond of children. Esther had gleaned that much when she caught the girl scolding Eric a couple of times when he was simply misbehaving as small children did.

When Finn and Will came into the dining room, both looked under the weather. "And what time did you get home last night?" Alma asked as she placed Will's breakfast plate in front of him. "I hope the pair of you did not get into mischief." Their mistress did not make a habit of coming into the dining room in the morning since they moved in here, so Alma had no qualms about speaking her mind.

"No, we did not," Will said as he sent Finn a wink behind Alma's back.

Esther glanced across at Finn, asking, "Will you now be making a habit of going off in the evenings?"

He seemed surprised at her question and merely shrugged. She did not get the chance to talk to him again until after lunch when she allowed the children time to play. Finn was in the final stages of building an enclosure for their few chickens who were currently being chased by Becky and Eric. Esther handed him a mug of tea and sat on the bench that he had also made.

"You are getting very handy," she said when he sat beside her.

"It is just a matter of banging a few nails into wood," he said. "I am no skilled carpenter I can assure you." Sipping his tea, he watched the young ones before saying, "It was not my plan to go into the dock area, I can assure you. Will got this idea into his head that I could make a few pounds by using my fists."

"And did you?"

"Hmm, as a matter of fact I did alright. Mind you, the other bugger had no skills and I got the feeling he had also been talked into fighting." For a while he sipped his drink. "The bloke who runs the whole shenanigans is keen for me to go back in a few days. I think he probably put the other fellow up against me so I would think I am onto a good thing. He will probably bring out his prizefighter next time."

Esther hesitated before asking, "Is this the life you wish for yourself, Finn?"

Seeming to be taken aback by her question, he scratched at an ear, before saying, "To be honest I have no plans, as for most of my life I had an uncertain future. When you live as I have you tend to take each day as it arrives." His mouth twisted before adding, "I'm as different from you as chalk from cheese, Esther. You now know almost as much about me as I know myself and must see that I am in no fit place to consider what type of future I wish."

The children tired of chasing chickens and came over to stand in front of them. "Chickens are fun," Becky said as she jumped up and down. "We have now given them good names." Eric and she began to reel off a string of ridiculous names and Esther did not have the heart to explain that soon most of the creatures would end up on their dinner plate. Without another word, Finn returned to his work.

As she took the children by the hand and walked back to the house, Finn seemed engrossed in his task and Esther got the feeling that he was either annoyed with her or vexed at her asking such a question of him.

The days seemed to slip past in a hurry as summer turned into autumn. Their mistress made no move to further their discussion about Esther's future. Finn was very busy each day with the many jobs needed inside and outside the house. He and Will went off on a few occasions, but she did not attempt to question him again on whether or not the expeditions had been worthwhile. When they did spend time together, their conversations were kept to impersonal subjects.

Finn had been given permission to ride Cecil Franklin's horse and so he and Will had taken to riding off on the evenings they went into the area of town where Esther guessed the fighting matches took place. His riding ability therefore improved. Sadly, for her, nothing else seemed to improve, and she began to feel melancholy at the thought of nothing changing in her life. Some nights she lay awake as she contemplated perhaps just taking Danny Boy and heading off. That foolish notion was soon quenched as she feared what could become of her out there alone. It was well known that bushrangers still ranged in the area.

A morning in June after a particularly cold few days when Finn had been asked to lay fires in all the hearths, the welcome sun streamed into Esther's room as she finished dressing, and an unusual ruckus came from the front hallway. She went straight to the room shared by the children to find both their small beds empty. As she descended the stairs to see what they were up to, Ruby came towards her looking quite flushed. "Where are Becky and Eric?" Esther asked the girl.

"Well, would you believe we have a visitor, and they came down still in their nightwear to see who it was. He's very handsome." She put her hands to her cheeks.

"But who would come calling at this early hour?" Without giving an answer, Ruby turned and jumped back down the remaining stairs.

Following her more slowly, Esther saw Mrs. Clements escorting a man into the parlour. She could see that he had hair as black as night and that he was tall. The children were nowhere in sight, so Esther went along to the kitchen. "What on earth were you thinking?" she scolded the two children who, still in their nightgowns, were eating their porridge.

Becky waved her spoon. "We were told to come in here by Aunt Priscilla. She told us to wait here until you came down. Guess what?" Without waiting for Esther's answer, she said with excitement, "Eric has an uncle, and he's come all the way down from somewhere far away."

Esther looked to where Alma was stirring the pot of porridge, and the cook merely shrugged and said, "Don't ask me. I didn't know she had any relatives hereabouts. She seemed very pleased to see him so that's nice for her. The poor woman has been through much tragedy that she deserves something nice to happen for a change." Will came in then followed by Finn. Both washed their hands at the sink before sitting at the table. "Did you know that the missus had a family member in the colony?" she asked Will.

With a shrug, he shook his head. "The fellow arrived last evening, apparently on the steamer from Sydney Town and has been staying at the hotel overnight. Said he didn't want to disturb the missus last night so late. She seemed excited by his arrival anyway."

"Perhaps she has an admirer," Finn said as he began to eat his porridge.

That thought had already entered Esther's head. Just then Priscilla came into the room followed closely by the newcomer. To match his very dark hair he possessed what Esther's Papa would call a swarthy skin. She judged him to be of similar age to Finn. He smiled around at everyone as their mistress said, "This is my dear husband's brother Lawrence, he will be staying here for a while. We will take breakfast in the dining room, if you would come along Alma and he will tell you what he would like." Turning, she left.

Before following her, the stranger smiled around at them all. His eyes seemed to linger on Esther for an instant longer and she felt a strange feeling in her chest. "So pleased to make your acquaintance," he said amiably, and it seemed as if the words were meant for her. "Please don't feel obligated to make any unnecessary fuss of me. I'm a simple chap who doesn't take well to being pampered." With that he sent them all a small salute before leaving.

"Well, I never, he's a rare sort, isn't he?" Alma said, before following him.

"I've never seen anyone so handsome," Ruby cooed.

Esther felt the same but was not about to agree with the girl. Instead, she turned to the children and told them to hurry and finish their porridge so that they could get dressed. "How lucky you are to have an uncle, Eric," Becky said. "I think I had one but he went away, and I didn't get to know him so my Mama told me." Esther stared at her in surprise for that was the first time she had mentioned either of her parents in all the time since that tragic day. It was as if she had fortunately blanked it out of her mind.

"He can be your uncle too," the boy said with a laugh.

As Esther rose, Finn said, "Being handsome don't always mean a person's any good, Ruby. I could tell you a few tales about some of the so-called nobs I have met, and they might look all nice and well-turned out, but believe me they usually have a nastier side beneath all their smiles and good manners. It doesn't do well to trust them."

Stunned by the fervor in his words, Esther shook her head, before ushering the children out. In the passage she met Alma, who said, "What a lovely young chap he is. Has lovely manners and didn't treat me like a servant."

Instead of reminding the cook that to her knowledge Alma had never been treated like a skivvy since she'd known her, as were none of the other staff here, Esther said nothing. In fact, Priscilla Clements was a fair mistress who never made them feel as if they were lesser people.

For lack of space elsewhere, a table had been set aside in the parlour for Esther to do the schooling. Mid-morning as she was testing mainly Becky on her adding and subtracting progress, the newcomer entered the room. With a small wave of the hand he said, "Ignore me please do. Priscilla is otherwise engaged, so I thought I would wander around the place." He glanced around the room before sitting in one of the easy chairs.

Feeling slightly perplexed Esther tried to carry on but her confusion got the better of her. Why this man had the power to make her feel so muddled she had no idea. When Becky stated, "Esther is a good teacher. I know all my letters and numbers now," she shushed her hurriedly.

"You are a bit on the young side, aren't you?" he said. "Where did you learn to be so clever? Did your parents hire a tutor?"

"My Papa was a medical man and my Mama a very intelligent woman. I learnt all that I needed to know from them." Esther had a feeling that her cheeks had gone rosy.

"You say he was, so is he not still in the medical profession?" Lawrence seemed really interested and not simply asking for the sake of making conversation.

Esther went on to explain as sketchily as possible how she lost them both not so long ago.

"What a sad tale. But you have obviously come through your ordeal and are managing to carry on with your life."

Was she? How he had managed to ascertain such on so short an acquaintance she did not know. But she said, "Not only were my parents very clever people, they also taught me to make the most of any situation." Wishing to steer the conversation away from her, she said, "You have also lost someone dear to you so know that we must go on as best we can. Tell me, did you come to the colony with your dear departed brother or at some other time?"

"Yes, we too lost our parents and me being younger, he in his wisdom brought me along when he received his sailing orders." Lawrence's mouth twisted slightly as he seemed to mull the situation over before adding, "I wish to blazes he had left me behind. I hate this hell hole of a place—and will return to England as soon as it can be arranged. How can you stand it here? I presume you came over with your family."

"Yes, but I was a four-year-old so had no say in the matter. To be honest, I know no other way of life, so it suits me well."

"But don't you ever yearn for the splendid life that can be had in any big city back there?" His hand jerked over a shoulder.

"As I say, I know nothing of life over there as you call it, so I make the most of what life brings me." Esther was not about to tell him that only recently she had brought the very subject of returning to their homeland up to Finn. While they had been talking, the children had taken the opportunity to leave the table and were busily playing a game in the corner of the room. "If you don't mind, Lawrence, I really must get on with their lessons."

"Oh yes, forgive me." Standing, he sent her a small salute and a wide smile before going out.

Esther walked over to the window, her feelings all of a muddle. If this man had thoughts of returning to England, then why had he made the trip down here? Becky interrupted her thoughts by tugging on her skirt, asking, "You are not leaving us, are you?"

"What on earth gave you that idea?" Esther took her by the hand and sat her back at the table.

"I heard you talking about it with that man that my aunt says is my uncle."

"Then you should not be listening to conversations that have nothing to do with you. It is bad manners. But to be honest with you, I am going nowhere." Deep down Esther had a feeling that was a slight fib, for she was beginning to realise that she wanted more out of life than she was currently getting.

Chapter Seven

Finn lay down the saw he had been working with and stared across the garden to where the newcomer was once again in conversation with Esther. His fists curled as he curbed the desire building in him to go over there this moment and plant one of his fists squarely on the finely shaped nose of this Lawrence bloke. How would the cove like it if that oh so perfect nose was flattened? Finn's confidence had risen after a few bouts where he had sent his opponent off with a bloody nose and at times even more, and he was convinced he could get the better of this man and send him packing.

So deep in his thoughts was Finn that he didn't hear Will approach. When his friend said, "The girl seems to be getting along fine with the newcomer," Finn's temper rose even more.

"Too well if you ask me," Finn snapped, then felt sheepish for his curt response.

Will stared at Finn for a while as if in thought, before saying, "Oh Finn, my old chum, I do believe you are jealous."

"Who me?" Finn pointed a finger at his own chin. "Wouldn't waste my time. If the silly chit wants to dally with the likes of that toff, then let her." He picked up his saw, but before he could set it to sawing, Will stopped him with a hand on his arm.

"Look, Finn, it seems that he is paying Esther some well-deserved attention. After all, let's face it, she's been through a mighty tough time and deserves to be treated like the lady she is. I heard a whisper that he is thinking of going off back to England and it is looking very much like he is trying his best to persuade the dear girl to accompany him." He turned as if to walk off but then said, "I also heard that the mistress is all for him taking the girl with him. It's also a fact that she probably arranged his visit for just that reason."

Finn shook his head. "That can't be true. Why would she want to lose the person who is looking after her children—and doing a fine job of it, plus a man who seems to be the only near kin she has left hereabouts." Deep down Finn felt that Will had likely hit the nail on the head. Hadn't he suspected Lawrence's arrival to be odd at this time, for why hadn't he visited before this?

When Will left him, Finn continued with his work, but his head buzzed with an anger that seemed to be building in him. Added to this, he had already felt that Esther was ignoring him since this new bloke's appearance. They had seemed to be getting on really well, but lately she barely passed the time of day with him. Sadly, the common-sense part of him knew that she deserved someone who dressed in fine clothes and had the manners of a gentleman, and certainly not an ex-con with barely enough money to get by on. Plus, one with an uncertain future.

Perhaps he had been kidding himself by thinking that she cared for him, if just a little bit. Her kindness had brought him into her life, so no doubt she now considered him a waste of time with no prospects of improvement. All of which was true.

When Lawrence sauntered back towards the house, Finn lay down his saw and strode across to where Esther now stood beside the small field where the horses spent most days. Placing his elbows on the fence beside her, for want of something to say he said, "Danny Boy is looking good these days."

Those beautiful eyes of hers seemed somehow sad as she nodded. "He is, isn't he? Perhaps I should take him out more. There never seems enough time though."

They leant on the fence in silence for a while—a silence that Finn thought seemed awkward on her part. Taking the bull by the horns so to speak, he blurted, "Is it true that you are thinking of going back to England with this Lawrence cove?"

Danny Boy wandered over to stand by them and Esther stroked his neck for a while before saying, "Not exactly. What is true is that he has asked me to accompany him. If you recall, I did mention that I had the idea of returning to my homeland and perhaps making the acquaintance of my scattered family."

"So, you did, but to be honest, I thought it was simply something that might happen sometime into the future." Rubbing his chin, Finn stared at a nearby tree where two koalas were taking a nap. "What of your horse here—you would think of leaving him behind?" He knew that sounded childish but then again knew that the horse meant a lot to her.

Resting her chin on her hands atop the fence she seemed to ponder this before saying, "You could look after him for me." She turned to stare up at Finn before adding, "Unless you made the decision to accompany me on my travels."

So astounded by that was he, that Finn simply gazed at her before saying, "And how would I manage that? You know I own simply what I have made with my fists, plus what I have earned from the missus—both of which do not amount to enough to pay my fare on a steamship to Sydney Town, let alone a sea journey to the other side of the world. Plus, I did say I have not the stomach for a long voyage."

After a long sigh when she gazed off across the small yard she said, "I must do more with my life, Finn, and my choices are limited. I could stay where I am, caring for children that are not my own, dreaming of another life I could have if I were daring enough to take the opportunity. I am unable to take such a step on my own. Like most women, I want children of my own and a husband that I can rely on to take care of me."

"And you think this Lawrence will fulfil those needs, Esther?" Just the thought of her going anywhere with him made Finn sick to the stomach. No use him daydreaming about a life with her, of giving her the home and the children she craved—not unless his life suddenly took a turn for the better. Or if he went out and robbed a bank.

"What other choices do I have? I think he is a kind person." Her shrug said that she was not entirely sure of that.

"You know that much about him on such a short acquaintance?" Deciding to spit out what had been niggling at him since the arrival of Lawrence, he dared add, "Do you not think it strange that this man suddenly appeared after you found out about your inheritance?"

Nibbling on the end of her thumb, she said nothing. Becky and Eric came towards them calling out her name, so Esther shrugged and went to meet them. Finn was left to wonder if perhaps the same notion had entered her head.

In the week that followed, Finn waited anxiously for Esther to bring the subject up again. Lawrence seemed determined to gain as much of her attention as was possible, even interrupting her classes with the children. On passing the room one morning, Finn heard the idiot reciting an amusing poem which made the children laugh.

When he entered the kitchen on his way back outside, Alma looked up from what looked like a pie she was preparing and said, "Looks like the young chappie is making headway with young Esther, don't it?" Finn could not tell whether she was jesting or truly meant the words.

"You think so?" he snapped, unable to keep his jealousy under control. "Surely she cannot be so foolish she will be taken in by his fancy clothes and worldly manner." He poured a mug of water from the jug Alma kept on the draining board and sat at the table to drink it.

"Well looks that way. The missus seems well pleased with her matchmaking, I think. And young Esther could do a lot worse."

"And she could also do a lot better." All his bad feeling came through in that comment.

"You think so? She isn't about to bump into anyone more suitable in this neck of the woods, young Finn." Halting her rolling of the pie pastry she sat opposite him. "Or perhaps you think you have a chance if you throw your cap in the ring, is that it?"

"Huh, what chance would I have—stupid ex-con with no skills except throwing a punch or two, and no prospects to speak of."

Alma sighed and returned to her pastry without any further comment, except to ask him to fetch water and wood for the stove. Later that night as he lay sleepless on his small cot in the stable, Finn went over the conversation with Esther and wondered what her answer would have been if he'd agreed to her offer to accompany her on the voyage to England. But what sort of man would that make him? It would mean he would be relying on her for every little thing—his travel ticket, his clothing, even the food he ate. After time, he would likely become a laughing stock amongst her well-to-do acquaintances once it became known that Finn was an ex-con with no prospects of gaining wealth of his own. He knew this often happened amongst the gentry, for Spence told him once that a lot of the so-called rich men only married some women for their dowry.

One of Finn's more unsavory jobs was to empty the chamber pots each morning, and he usually went into each room once the occupants had gone to the dining room or kitchen for their breakfast. A day or two after this conversation with Alma, he went into the room occupied by Lawrence since his arrival, and when he saw that person sitting on the side of the bed, he quickly turned to leave.

"It's all right, old chap, you can carry on doing the dirty work," Lawrence said with a laugh. "I'm ready to go down." As he reached the door where Finn still stood, he leant in close to ask, "Like fetching and carrying for us rich folk do you?" This he said with another of his laughs that was anything but pleasant.

The bucket Finn had in his hand held some pee and almost of its own accord it tipped slightly so that some of that pee went onto the highly polished boots of the toff. "So sorry sir," he said with as much malice as he could call up.

Lawrence's fist came up as his face showed its fury. Quick as a flash Finn set the bucket down and caught the fist with his left arm, bringing his right hand up with a swift punch to his attacker's jaw. The cove fell to the floor, so Finn poured more of the pee over his legs, stepped across his still body and went along to the next room.

Barely had he finished his rounds of the other rooms and gone down the stairs before the ruckus rose. In the time that he had known his employer he had never seen or heard her show a lot of emotion other than sadness at the loss of her brother, but when her shrieking began, he knew where this would lead. Deciding to dodge out the kitchen door, he ignored the comments and questions from Alma, Will and Esther as they all called out after him.

"Where is he?" he heard Priscilla Clements scream as he emptied the full bucket in the privy. A moment later she stormed through the kitchen door as he came out of the small shed. "What have you done?" she screamed at him with a raised fist. "My dear brother lies almost dead and tells me that not only did you raise a fist to him but also had the crude audacity to spill the contents of the bucket of waste over him.

You can get off the premises right now. I will not abide a brute such as you in my house."

The vehemence in her shrieking not only stunned Finn, but took him by surprise. "It will be a pleasure missus," he said, adding, "But I did not raise a fist to your so-called brother. It was the other way around, for I was simply defending myself. It was he who raised a fist to me."

"Stuff and nonsense," she shouted. "He is a gentle soul. Even if he did, and I do not believe it of him—I can only guess it was you who caused him to react with such bad manners."

Finn suppressed a laugh at that piece of nonsense. Dropping the empty bucket at her feet, he said, "I'll be off then, but if it pleases you, I would like to take my promised wages before I go."

"Wages? How dare you? Get out of my sight." So saying, she turned and marched back through the kitchen door where Esther, Alma, Will and Ruby stood, all looking shocked to the core.

Esther came across first, followed by Will, and the other two went back inside. "What on earth did you do, Finn?" Esther asked, looking shocked to the core. "I never thought to see her in such a rage."

"The cove asked for it," was all he could think to say to that, before turning to head for the stables.

Both she and Will followed him and as Finn began to stuff his few belongings into a sack, Will said, "Cool down lad, she didn't mean it I am certain. Don't know what you did to cause such a show of temper, but she will get over it."

"No, she won't, Will old friend, I went too far this time. I let my stupid temper get the better of me. That cove has been asking for trouble with me since he arrived, and I couldn't take it anymore. Besides, he was about to punch me first so I was just defending myself."

"You should have let it roll over you like water off a duck's back, Finn. He was intent on needling you for I reckon he was jealous."

"Jealous? Of me? Cripes, what did I do to make him jealous of me? A cove who has everything would hardly have cause to envy me, matey." Finn went back to stuffing the sack, wondering how much of the stuff he had accumulated he should take with him.

Esther put a hand on his arm, causing him to cease what he was doing. "For goodness' sake Finn, what on earth were you thinking?"

"What I was thinking, was that I am sick of the likes of his kind looking down their noses at a common bloke like me, treating us like dirt beneath their posh shiny boots. Just because they were born into wealth, they think they can treat us like horse shit beneath their feet."

"But where will you go, Finn?" She sat on his cot and stopped his hand. "I heard the mistress say she will not pay you the wages due."

"I'll get work. Worst come to worst, I can go to the docks and find something there. I have a few contacts now—and can always use my fists. That's about all I seem fit for." Pushing her gently aside he rummaged through the box that held his newly acquired clothes, wondering if it would be considered robbery if he took them.

Will turned and walked out, saying over a shoulder, "I'll go and see if the missus has calmed down. I don't think she will go through with it, Finn lad."

"Please reconsider, Finn," Esther said with a catch in her voice. "You're being hasty."

"Hasty? That's daft. She sent me packing. I poured pee over his nice breeches apart from giving him a bloody nose. He's lucky I didn't kill him."

Putting her head in her hands she muttered, "Stay here while I go and see what is happening." She rose and placed a hand on his arm before going out.

Finn sat on his cot and rubbed at his face. What a fine mess he'd got himself into this time. There was a small glimmer of pleasure beneath the worry over what he'd done to the posh cove. It was always on the cards that he would get himself into trouble one day with his fists. The shoulder that had caused him to land in hospital all those weeks ago began to ache as it did at times, and he wondered if he would be able to carry on with the fist fighting for any length of time.

Ah well, there was always work to be found at the docks. In fact, he'd been offered a job by a cove he met at the fights one night. He said that if Finn ever tired of the fist work, he could use a man such as he who was handy with his fists. At the time he hadn't taken a lot of notice, but now realised that he might end up seeking the bloke out. There was always a chance that there was something not quite right about this fellow, but Finn knew that he was in no position to quibble over such things.

Will came from the kitchen as Finn was about to leave. Handing Finn a package, he said, "Alma put some food together for you." He then delved into his pocket and pulled out a small wad of notes which he put into Finn's hand. "I made a fair bit out of your fights by backing you, matey, so take this to tide you over until you get work." He then surprised Finn by putting his arms about Finn's shoulders and giving him a brief hug.

"I can't take your cash Will." Finn tried to push the wad back at Will but he stepped away and shook his head.

"I'm not likely to be leaving this place mate, so you will need it more than me. Oh, and be warned, that bloke who offered you work at the docks—well, you watch your step there. I know for a fact that he mixes with the wrong kind." Without waiting for a response, he turned and hurried back to the house.

Finn stuffed the money deep into the pocket of his breeches where it sat alongside proof of his release from prison. Heaving the sack over his shoulder he stood looking at the house in the hope that Esther would come out to at least wish him farewell, but she didn't. Alma and Ruby stood there, both waving. Going over to the fence where all three horses stood as if watching the proceedings with interest, he gave Danny Boy a swift pat and then marched off, his heart feeling heavier in his chest than the sack he carried.

Making for the dock area as it really was the only place he knew where he would be most likely to find work of some kind, Finn kept going until he reached the public house where he had met the cove who arranged a couple of his fist fights. Plonking himself down on one of the stools by the bar, he ordered a glass of beer. He'd never really taken to that particular brew but had no idea what else to order. Like a lot of things, he knew little of the finer things in life. Pondering on the mornings' events he was still in a quandary over the behaviour of the missus. Could be, she had set her sights on Esther hooking up with her dead husband's brother, so perhaps she was pleased to have an excuse to toss Finn out and leave the field open for that cove.

As he swigged the ale, he looked around him at the odd mixture of customers. "Here for a bout?" the fellow behind the bar asked as he stood wiping at the scarred stretch of dark timber in front of him.

Finn shook his head. "Not tonight. I'm looking for work though if you happen to hear of anyone who wants a bloke who can put his hand to any job."

The bartender stopped his wiping and looked across the room, yelling out, "Hey Macduff, bloke here looking for work hereabouts."

Finn glanced over his shoulder. The man named Macduff was one of the largest blokes

Finn had ever come across, and he'd met many. Pushing his chair back until it tumbled to the floor behind him, he waved before lumbering towards the bar. Finn recognised him from a couple of his bouts and knew for a fact that he was a huge gambler who always seemed to be on a winner. His face bore many scars and Finn had a feeling that in his youth the man had also been a fighter. The beer-stained waistcoat he wore over a shirt that had seen better days attested to the fact that he may have a pocket full of cash, but he most certainly didn't spend it on fancy clothes.

"Well, well, it's Finn is it not?" he asked as he sat heavily on the stool beside Finn. "What'ya doing here on this fine day, lad? Looking for work you say? What kind? A man like you who is handy with his fists should stick to the fighting game."

"I was after something a bit more permanent. Fighting is not so bad but doesn't pay enough to keep a man in food and drink."

Macduff scratched at his huge belly and let out a guffaw. "Permanent work is hard to come by in this part of town if you don't have a trade. What you good at besides fighting?"

Finn had no idea how to answer that, for all he knew was fighting or sawing logs. He had done a short stint in the prison kitchens at one time but doubted that he could claim to be a good spud peeler. "I'm handy with a hammer," he lied, although he had built a pretty sturdy cage for the chickens. "Fact is I will put my hand to anything."

Scratching at his belly again, Macduff seemed to be pondering. "A fellow like you with the looks and all, is likely a favourite with the ladies, eh? How'd ya fancy a bit of light work in a brothel? I know of one where the mistress is on the lookout for a handy bloke who can keep an eye on the customers who get a bit ill-tempered at times—refuse to pay and that sort of thing. I know her usual fellow was carted off to the jail recently."

Finn stared at him as he considered that offer. "I would live there, would I?"

"I reckon." Macduff eyed Finn from collar to boots before roaring with laughter until his huge belly wobbled. "You'd probably have your choice of the ladies if it suited your fancy. A good-looking fellow such as yourself would make a nice change from the stinking sailors and dock workers who are the usual customers."

As Finn followed Macduff out of the public house after agreeing to give it a try, he contemplated how his life had taken such a weird turn lately. A stink of waste that likely came from the nearby rivulet filled the air. They didn't walk far before Macduff stopped outside a house where a large black cat sat in the patch of grass on the other side of a low fence. It stared at them as the big man ushered Finn through a gate. The house was not a lot different to the others along the street except this one had an upper floor. A few barefoot children in tattered clothes played in the yard of the house next door. Obviously used to the comings and goings of strangers, they ignored the two men.

Macduff knocked twice on a door in dire need of a coat of paint, and it was opened by a dwarf that looked to Flinn very much like a leprechaun he had seen years ago in one of the books stolen by a member of his gang. Except, he wore no hat. "Well, well, if it ain't old Macduff," he said in a squeak of a voice that matched his size. "What'ya doing here at this time of the day?"

"Is the boss lady available, Paddy?" As he asked this, Macduff rumpled the hair of the tiny fellow as if he was a child. It didn't seem to bother the leprechaun for he grinned amiably.

"Come on in, I'll fetch her. She usually takes a rest at this unearthly hour of the day, and won't be too pleased at being bothered so it had better be worth it." Before closing the door after them he looked up and down the street, and then shouted a few insults at the children next door about why they weren't off at the government school, which they responded to in the same vein. "Wait here." He then went along the passage to the rear of the house.

To Finn's surprise a scent of something he recognised as a perfume Mona Franklin had worn filled the air—a mixture of roses and soap. Paddy returned and gestured for them to follow him back along the passage where he opened a door and ushered them inside. The only time Finn had been in the close company of a woman of the streets was that one occasion many years ago, so he had no idea what was to come.

This woman sitting there looked to be not much more than perhaps fortyish. Her very large breasts almost surged out of the gown of some flimsy stuff that she had obviously pulled on hurriedly. Her face, although not ugly, bore signs of weariness. "This had better be good Macduff," she said, waving a hand their way for them to come closer.

"Ah well, Vera my love," he said with a grin. "I recall you said you were a' looking for a new strong lad to take some of the customers in hand when they refused to pay up or get too boisterous. This here is young Finn, the handiest fellow with his mitts that you will ever see. He's looking for work and a place to lay his head at night. I recommended your establishment."

"Oh, you did, did you?" Her eyes took in Finn from his head to his toes, before she added, "Well he looks fit enough. Got any serious diseases young Finn?" she demanded.

Taken aback, Finn shook his head. "Not that I know of miss."

"No need for that nonsense." She flapped a hand whose nails were painted red. "You can call me Vera, same as everyone else does." As if giving it a second thought she added, "We'll give it a try and see how things work out. Keep your hands off my girls and you'll do." With a wave towards the leprechaun she said, "He can sleep in the outhouse behind the scullery, Paddy. Show him where and then keep an eye on him." Looking to Macduff she said, "I'm off back to my bed, see you later, eh?"

Macduff grinned and saluted her, patted Finn on the shoulder and wished him good luck, before going back along the passage.

"Come on matey," Paddy said as he gestured for Finn to follow him. As they passed through the scullery, a bent old woman wearing an apron that covered her from shoulder to feet waved a spoon their way before continuing to stir whatever the huge pot on the stove contained. "That's Dotty," Paddy said, adding, "Dotty by name and dotty by nature." A loudish laugh followed what he thought must be funny. "Makes the best Irish stew in all the land."

Finn agreed that it smelt pretty tasty as Paddy led him into a small room that contained a proper bed plus a small chest of drawers. "Not the palace, but I hear the bed is comfy. You can stash your stuff in there." He gestured at the chest. "There's a pump outside the door there." He pointed back to the small scullery they had passed through. "And the outhouse is down the back."

After he left, Finn sat on the bed and not for the first time wondered what Esther thought of him leaving so suddenly—or even if she had even spared him another thought. What would she think of this new turn of events? With a sigh, he thumped on his knees and got up to unpack his sack. He cared not if the missus accused him of stealing as he stashed the spare pair of breeches and the shirt he'd brought along with him. In thinking, it probably made up for the loss of promised wages.

Chapter Eight

Esther sat on her bed and let the tears fall. What a disastrous turn of events. Since the arrival of Lawrence, she knew that Finn's dislike of the man had grown, but to do what he did had shocked her once she learned exactly what happened. Remorse hit her then as she regretted not at least wishing him farewell. What was he doing now and where was he? When she asked Will where he thought Finn had gone, he said that it was likely he'd made for the wharf area for he knew that part of town well now.

"But what will he do there?" she had asked and with a shrug Will told her that he was likely looking for the bloke who arranged the fist-fighting. Instead of bringing her some comfort this brought the opposite, as she fretted about what would then become of him. Alma told her in no uncertain terms that it was dangerous around that area of town, where sailors came off their ships and some drank themselves straight into their grave. How the cook knew this Esther had no idea and didn't ask.

After a sleepless night, Esther made a decision. No matter what happened in this house, she would follow Finn, if only to set her mind at rest that he was faring well. What a fool she was, to even consider Lawrence's stupid idea of returning to England with him. Although she had come to like him in a small way, she now had second thoughts on whether he was trustworthy, for she had heard a conversation between him and Priscilla Clements that made her almost certain that Finn had been right in not trusting his motives.

She was passing the parlour not long after Finn walked off and heard Priscilla say, "Well, that played out to our satisfaction, Lawrence. Now it is up to you to play it the right way, and the girl is yours."

"But I am still not sure if I have convinced her to accompany me anywhere, let alone to the other side of the world." For the first time he seemed to be unsure of himself.

"You are a man with a brain, or so I thought. Make the most of this opportunity while it is still fresh. It's the only chance you will get to find someone who is better off by far financially than yourself. If you hadn't squandered the bequest endowed to you by your brother, you would not be in this particular position."

"I told you; I made a poor decision on an investment is all." To that Priscilla simply snorted.

After dressing and preparing the children for the day, Esther went into the kitchen. If she followed through with her decision, she would be leaving Becky who she had become fond of. But the girl seemed more than happy to be sharing her life here with the boy that she now called brother. Priscilla might not be the most caring person, but Esther was certain that she would always treat Becky as best she could, if only because she had so obviously loved her ill-fated brother.

When Will finished his breakfast, Esther told the children to go along to their desk and she followed Will out. He was brushing his favourite horse when she approached him. Nibbling on her thumb she drew up the courage to ask, "Will, would you kindly harness my Danny Boy up for me as I have made the decision to leave this place."

For a moment he seemed taken aback but then shook his head. "Following the young fellow, are you? I had I feeling you might."

"When Lawrence was showering me with so much attention, I had a feeling that Finn was jealous. I am sorry to say that I foolishly ignored his warnings."

"Found out the truth, did you?" Will placed the brush aside and with a slight push headed her towards the stable. Once inside he said, "Are you sure about this leaving though? It's a tough world out there for a woman alone, especially if you are going to where I am certain Finn headed. What happens if you can't catch up with him?"

"I heard them talking." She gestured towards the house. "Seems Finn saw what a schemer Lawrence was, but silly woman that I am, I took no heed."

"Yes, he told me of his thoughts. But what if Finn doesn't want to be found? What will you do then?"

"If I am in that predicament, I will continue on my way to the town called New Norfolk. My Papa told me of this place. There is a hospital there and the town even has a post office. If I am left with no other choice, I will seek employment at the hospital. Papa taught me many things about illnesses and diseases, I am sure I can offer assistance there."

Will scratched at his head. "Looks as if you have thought this through, Esther. But I still have many doubts. I have an idea. What if I come along with you, just so you are not alone in this venture? I have messages to run for the missus." Rubbing his chin, he glanced towards the house. "The fellow Lawrence has just come out and looks very much like he will be heading this way. You go on and meet him, and best not let on your intentions. Have no fear, I will have your cart ready to leave in no time and even pack some grain for Danny Boy just in case you need it.”

Esther wanted to reach out and kiss him for his kindness but there was no doubt that Lawrence was intent on catching her. Giving her a broad smile, he held out a hand in greeting. “Ah, there you are, the children are causing a stir and Priscilla wondered where you had wandered off to at this early hour.” Taking her hand, he steered her towards the kitchen door.

“I was just checking on my horse,” she lied as she tried unsuccessfully to drag her hand from his firm grip.

“Ah, so that was why you were in such deep conversation with the driver.” With another smile that she sensed was false, he continued, “I was wondering if you have given my suggestion any more thought. The next sailing for the homeland is in four weeks so I will need to go ahead with the details involved.”

Taken aback by his presumption that she was anywhere in the process of making a decision on voyaging with him, she tried again and this time managed to release her hand. “I have given it no more thought,

Lawrence. At no time did I give you my assurance that I would consider travelling with you. I thought it was simple idle chatter.”

That made him annoyed. He tried to conceal it, but she sensed anger boiling somewhere inside him. “Well, I thought we had come to an amicable agreement. You did seem to make it clear that you might wish to go back at some stage to find lost relatives.”

“Certainly I did, but that was in the future, and certainly not in four weeks’ time. Now if you will excuse me, I must get on to the children’s lessons.” His face and demeanor showed that he was trying his utmost to conceal rage as she turned and walked away.

Instead of going to the children, Esther went straight up to her room, where she pulled out the few dresses and other articles of clothing that her employer had given her. For a moment she considered leaving everything and just going with what she had come into this employment with, but then changed her thinking. The promised wage had not been received so far and no mention had been made of it, so perhaps a few dresses, underthings and a jacket and wrap would take the place of payment. An inbuilt pride wanted her to leave everything, but as she had no notion of where she was going or how things would work out, she decided it best to at least be prepared in some small way for any occurrence.

Once she had her Papa's precious satchel and the few other items packed into a small travelling bag she had also been given before they moved, she glanced around the room while pondering whether or not to say her goodbyes. Good manners would not allow her to leave in such a way though, as Priscilla Clements had been kind enough to give her a home after the fire.

With the bag in her hand, she went down to the sitting room where she guessed her employer would be writing or doing her embroidery. After her soft tap was answered with a, "Come in," she entered. Lawrence was there with Priscilla and by the look on her face he had already disclosed what Esther said to him earlier. "Esther, my dear." Priscilla gestured for her to move closer. "What is this I hear about you refusing dear Lawrence's kind offer of travelling with him?"

"Madam, I had no intention of going anywhere with him, and if he mistook my interest in the topic for agreement, then I apologise sincerely." Esther placed the bag on the carpet and moved closer but kept her distance from Lawrence. "I have made the decision to move on and hereby tender my resignation."

The shock on Priscilla's face would have been amusing if this was in any way a laughing matter. "Move on? But where will you go, my dear?" It was clear that she fought an urge to yell and scream, and Esther was momentarily shocked at the change from her previously calm demeanor.

"Can you not see, dear Priscilla, she is going to join that scum that you gave a home to when he had nowhere else to go," Lawrence said with a nasty curl to his lip. Moving closer to Esther, who backed up a step or two, he shouted, "And to think I mistook her for a respectable woman. She is no better than him it seems."

For a brief moment Esther felt the urge to retaliate and let him know that in her opinion Finn was by far a better man than he, but then a sense of relief hit her for he had now made it easy for her to walk away from this pair. Without another word, she turned her back on them, retrieved the bag, and marched out of the room with head held high.

When she faced the children with the news that she was going on a journey and might never see them again, Eric showed little interest. This did not surprise Esther for she had come to realise that the boy lacked much enthusiasm for life in general. Becky on the other hand began to howl. "You cannot leave me I need you," she screamed.

"Who will look after me now?" she added in a childish whimper.

"You have Ruby, Becky. She loves you." Esther knelt in front of her and pulled her close. "And your aunt loves you dearly." Putting her away, Esther stood. For a moment remorse hit her, for she pitied this child who might perhaps one day recall the nightmare of that awful day when her parents died. After a swift kiss on Becky's cheek, she went out and shut the door.

As she passed the sitting room Lawrence was still ranting on. Alma had obviously overheard at least part of the goings on, for as soon as Esther entered the kitchen, she pulled her close and whispered, "You're doing the right thing, girl. I could have told you that Lawrence only showed his face here when she sent him news of your good fortune. Even after she lost her dear husband soon after arriving in this part of the colony, he didn't bother coming to offer comfort."

"Please ensure that Ruby takes good care of Becky. I would dearly like to take the child with me, but fear that would be a crime, for Mrs. Clements is her legal guardian now. Besides, I have no idea what the future will hold for me."

"I'm sure things will work out fine for you." Alma patted Esther's hand. "You go and find that Finn fellow—the lad may not be a nob, but he is made of solid stuff is that one." Giving her a slight push, she said, "Now get away with you and find yourself a good life girl. One where you are not at the beck and call of the likes of her in there."

Will was waiting beside Danny Boy. "I will come along aside you," he said as he took her bag and placed it behind the bench. "I can walk home. I just want to make sure you are settled somewhere safely."

"Thank you, Will, that's kind of you." Esther knew that it would not take much more to bring her to tears. He assisted her up and without looking back, Esther guided Danny Boy out onto the road.

"I've put some grain in back there, just to tide you over," he said as they jogged along. "Now, I have a feeling Finn would have headed for a certain drinking house near the wharf, so I reckon we go there first."

The streets were very busy, with carts and carriages going about their business. It did not take very long to reach this public house. After Will helped Esther down, he said, "Perhaps it will be best if you leave me to ask about Finn." He beckoned to a couple of lads who were staring at them from where they lounged against the wall. "Look after my property and I'll see you all right when I come back," he said.

A few men of unsavory appearance stared at Esther, making her feel uneasy, so she was extremely grateful that Will had agreed to come with her. How she would have found the courage to enter this establishment had she come alone, she had no idea. Although used to seeing many convicts and poorer people while her Papa went about his business both in Sydney Town and here, she had never had to face them without her Pa. It hit her that she had not thought ahead to how she would cope with searching for Finn alone.

The bar was filled with smoke from the many pipes, and the stench of unwashed bodies mixed with beer made her feel quite sick. Intent on not showing her fear she held her head high and kept as close to Will as was decent as he neared the long bar, behind which a jovial man was serving the few men who lined up in front of it.

Will stood while the barman finished serving and when he gave Will a salute and greeted him, Will asked about Finn. "Ah you want to speak to old Macduff. The bloke you are asking after went off with him. Dunno where they went from here though." With a glance about the noisy room, he gestured with the hand holding a not too clean piece of rag. "That there's who you're after. The big 'un in the corner yonder."

Will thanked him and as they headed to where he had indicated, a couple of the men shouted rude remarks at Esther, making her wish she had stayed outside. Once Will was assured that he was indeed speaking to Macduff, Will asked, "I was told you might be able to direct me to where a young fellow named Finn went after leaving here. Tall bloke with hair the colour of sand."

As the big man's eyes settled on her, Esther moved behind Will. "And who might be after him?" he asked.

"I'm a good friend of his and came here along with him a few times when he took part in some bouts."

"Oh aye, and who might be the sweet little lass you have along with you?" With a chuckle, he added, "Not the sort of lassie we usually see in these parts I must say."

"I dare say," Will replied. "But as it happens, this lady is the one who seeks him—has some very important news to impart to him. It's rather urgent that we find him as soon as possible."

Scratching at his large belly he seemed to ponder this before saying, "Hmm, now let me think." Esther had a feeling that he did not need to do any thinking but knew quite well who Finn was and exactly where he had gone. "Now then, the young fellow was looking for employment so I took him along to Vera's place. She runs a nice establishment and was looking for somebody just like him." With a glance at Esther, he added, "Best not take the lady there though, me lad." To this advice he added a nudge to Will's arm. "Now, you don't have to go far." He then gave Will a few directions, adding, "Can't miss it, as it is the only house with two floors along that part of the road."

"Thanks kind sir," Will said, catching Esther by the arm. "Good day to you."

As they walked towards the door, a man who looked as if he had drunk more than his share of liquor, caught at Esther's skirt and she reeled back in fear. "Spare a copper for a poor old bloke down on his luck, miss. It ain't fer me," he slurred. "It's fer me poor old missus an' kids."

Esther wanted to tell him that in that case he should be home caring for them and not here drinking himself into an early grave, but Will delved into his coat pocket and tossed a coin onto the table. "Take that and get home right now to your family."

The cool air was refreshing after the stuffy stink of the bar. Esther breathed a sigh of relief to see that Danny Boy was still there. The young lad stroking his nose, said, "He's a nice one is he, always wanted one of me own I did." He then held out his hand.

As Will dropped a coin into it, Esther said, "I must repay you, Will. I never thought of such details when I made the decision to leave."

Will shook his head. "No problems, young Esther. It is merely a coin or two." As Will helped her onto the cart bench, Esther was also relieved to see that the bag she had brought with her was still safely in the back. "The afternoon is wearing on, so perhaps it might be best to ensure you have somewhere to rest this night. I think before we seek out Finn, we should go to the hotel which is just along the next street. Perhaps you are also feeling in need of refreshment."

Esther agreed. Her sleepless night was catching up with her and what she needed more than anything, apart from finding Finn, was to rest awhile. Once Will had ensured that she was sure of a place for her to spend the night, he said, "Perhaps it might be best if you stay here now, and I will go in search of Finn. I really need to get back or there will be a ruckus as they wonder where I have been for so long. I'll ensure he knows where to find you."

"Thank you Will, and I cannot find the words to tell you how much I appreciate your assistance."

Once he left, Esther sat on the bed and let out a sigh. The room was not sumptuous but was comfortable, and she felt safe. Putting her head in her hands she let a few tears fall. More than likely fatigue had made her feel so sad and lonely. New doubts began to fill her as she contemplated a life alone if Finn decided he had no desire to seek her out. Thankfully, Will had assured her that Danny Boy was safely settled in stables nearby where she felt certain he would be taken care of.

A young girl brought her a meal of roast meat and vegetables and a jug of hot water so she could refresh herself. Once Esther had eaten and bathed her face and hands, she took off her boots and lay down on the bed. But restless, she soon rose and went over to the window that overlooked the street where the people of the town were going noisily about their business. The afternoon was drawing to a close when the young girl who had brought her meal tapped on the door with a message that she had a guest who was waiting down in the parlour.

Esther quickly pulled on her boots, straightened her hair, and went down the stairs, with butterflies flitting about in her stomach. Finn stood by the window, his back to the door as she entered. Curbing the strong desire to rush to him and put her arms about him, she coughed.

"Esther, what on earth made you come here?" he said as he faced her. "Thank the lord Will came along with you." There was no pleasure in his features and for a brief moment she wondered herself what had convinced her that this would be a good idea.

"I couldn't stay there," she said, feeling much like a schoolgirl facing her tutor. "Lawrence was convinced that I was willing to voyage with him back to England, and I had no desire to do that."

Rubbing at his eyes, Finn shook his head. "This is not wise, nonetheless. What did you plan on doing next?" Esther had the distinct feeling that he found her presence here a nuisance rather than a pleasant surprise.

With a shrug, she confessed, "To be honest, my only plan was to seek you out to see if you would be willing to travel with me. I have decided to perhaps go to New Norfolk. I have heard that it is a thriving town." She sank onto a nearby chair. "No doubt you have already found employment and are seemingly content there."

"Well, yes, I have found work, but I would not say that I am content there. It was the best on offer—and I was in no position to pick and choose." He sat on the nearest chair to hers and stared down at his hands as they rested on his knees. "Esther, you must see that I cannot travel with you. I am nothing more than an ex-convict and you are a lady of means now. You can go wherever you please and do whatever you wish, but I am and will always be a penniless man."

Esther went onto her knees in front of him and took his hands in hers. "You are the only person I can trust, Finn, I have no one else. I may as you say have means, but have little besides except perhaps Danny Boy. We certainly met under unusual circumstances, but I felt that you were trustworthy. And you have proved me right. You could have absconded at any time, but you did not, so tell me Finn, why did you stay?"

That question seemed to have taken him by surprise. "I stayed because I also have no one else. Like some angel you came along when I was in need of help. But Esther, I had just been given my release from prison so I would have been a fool not to accept your offer." He stared down at his work-worn hands for a while. "For all you know I could have told you a heap of lies."

"But you didn't, you have told me everything about your early days."

Shaking his head on a deep sigh, he said, "Esther, I really have not a lot of idea who I am really. Even my name was picked out of a book. The only part of my past that I know for a fact is true is being taken to London by some rich woman who thought to do me a justice. As it worked, out that was a disaster.

You cannot turn a pig's ear into a silk purse." With a small laugh he added, "That was told to me by one or two members of the gentry before I ran away to be with my own kind, living by our wits on the streets."

"All this was no fault of yours." Rising, Esther went back to sit, before saying, "The way I see things is that we are two people who are now alone in the world. We have nobody to worry about or care whether we stay or go, so why do we not make a life for ourselves of our choosing? You could even pick another name and a story to suit." Esther rubbed at her face, feeling very weary suddenly. "I feel as if I am begging—but if that is the case, then perhaps I am. You are the only person—except for Will of course—who has really worried about me for whatever reason."

Rising he went over to stare out of the window, hands thrust into the pockets of his breeches. "The employment I found is at a place where no decent woman would enter. It seems that the fellow Macduff thought it suitable for someone such as me who was only good at using his fists. My job there is to keep the male customers in hand. Perhaps you know nothing of these places, Esther, but it is where women, and one is probably not even a woman yet, well they give their bodies for money, do you understand?"

Esther shook her head and went to stand at his side. "I know little of these places, of course. But I did overhear my parents talking of such a one before we came down this way. A girl had given birth and as my Papa was working nearby, he was called to assist. I heard them saying that the baby died because the place where it was born was filthy and the poor girl wretched."

Placing his hands on her shoulders, he stared down at her before saying, "If I do come along with you, Esther, what would people think of you—a young well brought up woman does not befriend a man such as myself. We would have to create another lie, and honestly, I am sick of lying. I would not want you to be brought down to my level."

"I have an idea, Finn. We could get wed. That would solve everything. Travelling as a married couple we would cause no confusion or questions."

Finn stared at her before asking, "Married? To me? You are aware of what being married means are you not? You would then be tied to me, in truth for life, and I would have complete control of everything in our lives from that moment on."

"Of course, I know. My parents were a good example of what it means to share your life with another."

Chapter Nine

Finn strode along the street in a daze. Could he really have consented to marry Esther? What possessed her to think that he was worthy of spending his life with such as her? He'd left her with a promise to return the next morning, prepared to go along to the nearest minister and be wed. All he had to do now was tell Vera of his intentions.

"Where do you think you've been?" Vera bellowed as soon as he entered the house. "We are heading to our busiest time, and you take it into your head to go off gallivanting. You are here to look after my girls, and that's what you will do, fella." With a wave of the hand, she turned to smile and simper to a customer who stood by the door.

About to tell her of his plan to leave as soon as this man was settled with his girl of choice, a ruckus from the floor above caught his attention. Paddy came from the back room and waved a hand Finn's way. "Best go see what that's all about," he said.

With a sigh, Finn took the stairs two at a time, reaching the top just as a man came from the room where a woman's scream echoed across the hallway. "Pig," she yelled. "That ain't the way to treat a lady." Finn noted blood streaming from a place above one of her eyes, just at the moment he recognised the woman's assailant.

"Well, look who it is." Lawrence said with a sneer twisting his mouth. "Just exactly where I expected you to end up." Looking over his shoulder he shouted, "Shut up, you silly cow, you are no lady."

"And you are no gent," Finn yelled as he brought his fist up, aiming for the bastard's chin. Lawrence forestalled him by giving him a mighty push that sent Finn tumbling backwards. His head hit the stairs and he heard women screaming and Paddy shouting in his funny little voice before everything went black around him.

"Come on lovey, wake up." One of the girls was mopping his face with a damp rag, but Finn could not work out which one it was, for his eyes could not seem to focus. She dabbed at his brow, which ached something awful, and the sudden pain that shot up through the shoulder he'd injured before told him that once again it had been bashed out of place.

"What happed?" Finn asked croakily. "Why am I lying here?" He tried in vain to push himself into a sitting position, but gave up when the pain worsened.

"That bastard bloke gave Mildred a whopping black eye. He took off after he knocked you down the stairs. Refused to pay too, so Vera ain't happy." She dabbed again at his face. "Looks like you are going to have a lovely shiner tomorrow."

Finn dashed the dabbing hand away and with difficulty pushed himself up. The pain that shot through his arm and shoulder was ten times worse than previously, and when he saw bone in the low part of his arm at a funny angle, he had a feeling something in there was broken. Once he'd seen a cove with a broken bone and this looked to him very much like it.

"Oh gawd," he heard Vera moaning in the background somewhere. "Get him out of sight will you. The customers are waiting." She clapped her hands. "Put him in my room for now." Saying that she scurried away to greet a couple of men who stood in the hallway.

It took three of the girls plus Paddy to shuffle him along the passage. Finn had never felt so out of control, even when getting knocked unconscious once in a fist fight. The pain was enough to make him want to scream like a babe, and even his head hurt. Once they had him by Vera's bed, they managed somehow to get him on it. For a moment he felt sure he had blacked out again, for when he opened his eyes the girls had gone and Paddy was saying, "I'll have to get a boy to run for the doctor. Just let's get your boots off."

Finn lost all track of time as he lay in agony. He had no idea how long it was before a stooped old man arrived and introduced himself in a strange dialect as Doctor Bradley. After ordering Paddy to fetch his patient a dram of whiskey he set about first pushing Finn's shoulder back into place. Thankfully all went black again then, for when Finn awoke there was a funny contraption on his lower arm. The doctor was nowhere in sight and when Paddy poked his head around the door Finn cried, "What the hell is this thing?" He tried in vain to lift the arm. "And where's that Doctor bloke gone?"

Paddy came across and tapped the sort of box around Finn's arm. "Doc said it is called a splint, and it will hold the bone in place until it heals. First off, he bound it and then put some white stuff on that he said would make it hard, before strapping it up like this using these bits of timber. Clever bloke ain't he, said he learnt how to do it in his old homeland. Not sure where that was but he spoke funny."

"How long do I have to keep this thing on?" Finn wiggled around so that he could put his feet to the floor. Realising he still had no boots on, he demanded, "Where's my boots?"

"Now calm down. Here's your boots. He suggested you rest as much as you can to let it heal faster, and he also said you have a nasty gash on your head—and you will likely have what he called a concussion or something. Anyway, he said you should take it easy. Vera is in a right fit. Says you have to get to your own bed as soon as you can. At least your legs don't seem any the worse for wear. She's talking of chucking you out for you aren't much good to her like this, so I suggest you keep out of her way for a day or so."

"Day or so? I have to go right now, Paddy. I came back to tell her I am going. Would you believe I have a girl waiting for me? Wants to marry me so she says." Finn made to stand but had to flop back down when his head seemed to whirl around on his shoulders.

"Looks to me as if you aren't much good in your present state for any girl who is silly enough to want to wed you." Paddy's chuckle softened his chide. "What possessed you to take to that bloke anyway? Vera says she took you on to protect the girls but not to punch the blokes. You should have just escorted him out the door, but making sure he paid his due cash first. If we go around chucking the customers out just because they get a bit handy, we'd end up with nobody. The girls are used to being manhandled; I don't know what the silly bitch was making such a fuss over anyway."

"You don't know? Well, that makes you as bad as Vera. I might seem a rough sort, but I do know that no woman deserves to be treated badly. And anyway, I know the bloke and he's a no-gooder let me tell you." Finn made another effort to rise but was forced to realise that he would not be going anywhere just yet. Certainly not while he had this cage thing on his arm. "When did this doctor say I can get rid of his splint?"

Paddy shook his head. "Didn't say. I know a bloke who did the same thing, and he had to put up with it for weeks, so I wouldn't plan on going off just yet. He also gave you something that he said would help you with the pain, said it might make you a bit sleepy." With a small wave he went out when he heard Vera yelling for him.

Finn lay fretting as he wondered how he could get a message to Esther. Sometime latter Paddy came back along with the Scot Macduff, and between the two of them they somehow managed to get Finn along to his own bed. After a few words of stern telling-off, Macduff went off.

When Finn next opened his eyes, the sun was up and sending a beam from the small window across the bed. Needing to relieve himself, he somehow managed to shuffle out to the outhouse and with difficulty do what needed to be done. After quickly sluicing his face and hands at the pump as best he could, he went back to sit on his bed, where he looked about for his boots. As he tried to pull one on, his head began to spin again so he lay back and closed his eyes.

Paddy shook him awake, and with bleary eyes Finn saw that the sun no longer shone into the room. "What time is it?" he wondered as he twisted and put his feet to the floor.

"The girls have been working for a while so it must be about midnight." Paddy handed him a bowl, saying, "Dotty sent you some stew—thought you would be hungry. That stuff the doctor gave you must have been a strong brew; you've slept for a long time. The girls were getting worried about you. Wanted to come in to make sure you are not dead."

"Hours?" Finn cried. "You mean I have been out all day? No, I have to go, I told you. There's someone waiting for me." He placed the bowl on the floor and stood, shakily taking the few steps across to the hook that held his jacket. With a curse he realised he didn't have a hope of pulling it on while in this state.

Paddy took the coat from him and placed it on the bottom of Finn's bed. "Don't be daft, matey, you are not in a fit state to be going anywhere, least of all chasing after some wench. If she really cares for you, won't she wait awhile? At least eat the stew, it'll help you to build up your strength to face her."

Seeing the sense in that, Finn sat again, placing the bowl on his knees. The stew was tasty and he realised he hadn't eaten or drunk anything for hours. Paddy left him alone and he went over the situation, trying to be sensible. Could be that the dwarf was right and if Esther really cared then surely she would realise that something was amiss and wait around a bit.

What did he know of women anyway? He had no idea if she really cared or if she just needed a man around for protection on her travels. Following on from that thought was that she did seem to be serious about them getting wed. Thoughts and doubts whirled about in his aching head as he dozed again.

When he awoke, sun streamed into the dingy room and as he sat up his head whirled again. "Paddy," he yelled, but the dwarf did not appear for a while and Finn must have dozed again.

Paddy shook his shoulder. "Sorry, mate, was cleaning up. We had a busy night. How you feeling?"

"Still not up to scratch." Finn put his feet to the floor, knowing deep down that he had no hope of going off to find Esther while in this state. "Would you do me a favour Paddy," he asked. When Paddy nodded dubiously Finn said, "If you can get out, would you mind going round to the hotel and asking for a lady named Esther..." He had to think a while for could not remember her other name. "Think she is Miss Blythe," he said. "Tell her what a mess I am in and ask her to wait around for me until I can get up and about a bit more."

Scratching at his chin Paddy nodded after giving it a bit of thought. "All right. I'll go but I can't get out for now. Soon as I can get away, I will go."

When he had gone, Finn went out to the outhouse and stayed outside for a bit in the sunshine as he fretted again on whether Esther would be waiting for him. Later, one of the girls brought him a dish of beef stew and when he asked after Paddy, she said he had gone out for a bit, and she didn't know where. She also advised him to keep well out of Vera's way.

When Paddy shook him awake from a deep sleep, Finn sat up too fast and his head felt as if it was spinning on his shoulders. "What did she say?" he cried as he grabbed Paddy small hand.

Paddy's mouth twisted as he shook his head. "She wasn't there, old mate. The bloke gave me this." He took a small pouch from a pocket and handed it to Finn. "He said that if you turned up, he was to give it to you. Wasn't too keen on handing it over, but I convinced him I was up front when I told him of your plight. He said the lady did not look happy."

With trembling fingers Finn opened the pouch which he saw contained a folded piece of paper and also a bank note. The message said, "I am sorry I could not wait around longer Finn, but decided to start out on my journey to this place called New Norfolk. The innkeeper here assures me that there is a reputable hotel there called The Bush Inn and that is where I shall wait awhile should you decide to join me. If you do not, then please accept the enclosed and I wish you blessings in the future, regards Esther."

Finn stared down at the words and then again at the pouch containing the note with the bank details on it. In all his life he had never possessed money so had no idea of its worth. "I have to go, Paddy. Can you help me out of this thing." He raised the arm holding the contraption.

Paddy shook his head. "Oh, not so sure about that, Finn old boy. It's not a good idea. Medical man said you should keep it on for a long time. Look, if she took the trouble to send you this, then I reckon she is intent on waiting around a while for you. Where did she say she was heading?"

"To a town they call New Norfolk. She said she was going to stay at the inn there. But I doubt if she will stay around too long. Don't you see, Paddy? I can't stay here anyway; Vera will be tossing me out on my ear soon enough if I can't work."

"That's a fact." Paddy rubbed at his chin. "Just give it another night, then I'll help you fix up the arm as best I can. There's a coach leaves for that town—not sure if it's every day, but I heard that is a good place to settle. Even if she decides to move on you can likely find yourself work there."

"Not with this thing strapped to me I won't." Finn wondered if Paddy had looked into the pouch before handing it over and if he was aware that Esther had provided him with likely enough to get by on. "All right, I'll hang around one more night. Can you find out when the coach leaves next, Paddy?"

"Good fellow. I'll do that, and you take it easy while you can. It isn't likely to be easy once we get rid of the splint thing." Paddy left him and Finn re-read the note, and marveled at Esther's generosity. She had shown him nothing but goodness and kindness since their first fortunate meeting. Could she see something in him that he was not aware of himself, or was she simply a foolish trusting woman?

Two days went by with Finn swinging between sleeping and fretting. The pain seemed to be easier, but that was likely due to him resting the arm so much. A door slamming made him jump soon after he finished the plate of porridge brought by the lass that he defended that fateful night when his future was cruelly turned upside down. "You!" Vera stood by the open door with an accusing finger pointed at him. "I want you out and gone—right now." Her shout could likely be heard two streets away. "You've sponged off me long enough and done nothing to earn your bed and food, so get your things together and march."

Her anger did not surprise Finn, for he'd been waiting for this order. Placing the bowl aside he stood and bent to pick up his bag without a word. The door slammed shut as she left and a few moments later Paddy came in. "Well, s'pose it was to be expected, eh. To be honest I heard her moaning about you yesterday. She's taken another bloke on, and he will need the bed."

"I was waiting for it anyway, Paddy. Can you tackle this thing?" Finn lifted the arm with the dreaded splint. "I won't look so much like a useless bugger once I get my coat on to cover it."

"I'll go get a knife to cut the bindings." He turned for the door but then said, "But it isn't gonna be easy without it. I reckon you won't be much use to yourself, let alone anyone else for a while."

Paddy's words proved true, for as Finn strode along the street an hour later, his arm ached fit to drop off and felt strange with the stiff bindings around it. First stopping place was in Macquarie Street. Stopping outside the imposing bank building, his thoughts returned to the day he'd come here with Esther. Perhaps the manager or whoever dealt with her that day would remember him being aside her. But when he handed the banknote to the man on the other side of a counter, the man looked at him as if he was a likely robber. Told rather sternly that he must prove his identity, Finn took out the only means he possessed of proving that— his treasured document from the Commissariat's office.

When the man handed over ten pounds to Finn, there was a touch of what Finn thought might be regard as he said, "Well, well, your lady must be a wealthy benefactor or perhaps this is your wages for the past six months labour."

Having no answer for that, as Finn secured the treasure deep into the pocket of his breeches, he asked, "Could you direct me to the coach station please sir?"

As luck would have it, on reaching the coaching station he was told one would be ready to leave in a short time, so he sat alongside a man and his wife who seemed to be in bad temper with their boy, who sulked. For all they did not seem happy with life, Finn envied the man. What would it feel like to be wed to a woman and for her to bear your child, he wondered as he tried to chide the boy out of his sulks by pulling a face at him. The boy turned his back, perhaps through shyness.

They and he were joined by an old man who fell instantly asleep after nodding Finn's way once the coach was on its way. The scenery was pleasant with the afternoon sun sending a warmth over the countryside. Finn joined the old man after a while and slept, likely because he was aching from his head to his rear end. The boy shouting with glee woke him and he saw that they were alongside the river heading towards the buildings of the town.

After asking for directions to the Bush Inn Esther mentioned, he set out to find it hoping that she was still here and had not decided to move elsewhere. On entering the inn, he saw a young woman who looked to be a maid and beckoned to her. When she asked, "Can I help you sir?" he felt quite the gentleman.

"I am expected by Miss Esther Blythe. The lady asked me to meet her here," he said as he placed his bag on the floor.

"Oh yes, sir." With a small curtsy she added, "Just wait here and I will fetch the lady. Lovely girl she is." With a cheeky smile she ran off along the corridor.

Within a few moments Esther appeared, and at the sight of her, for the first time in his life Finn felt as if his heart was about to burst in his chest. He curbed a desire to pull her into his arms and hold her tight.

"Finn, you made it. Did you have any trouble finding the inn?" Her face showed no sign of whether she was pleased to see him or not. "I was worried that you decided to move on elsewhere."

"Well, like an idiot I had a silly accident—my own fault entirely." Finn went on to explain how his arm had become broken, but for some reason did not mention the name of the man who caused his fall. He brought his injured arm up and said, "I broke this, so the medical man said, and he put it in a contraption called a splint. I left that behind, but it is well bound."

"Oh, you poor man." She moved closer and for a moment Finn thought and hoped that she would throw her arms about him. "I know what you mean. Papa once told me how he mended someone's arm in the same way. When did this happen?"

"After I left you. I was quite poorly for a day or so as I also bashed my head, so was not fit for anything."

"Well, you are here now. We will speak to the innkeeper to ensure you are made comfortable and you must rest for as long as it takes until you feel better." She beckoned for him to follow her into what he thought was the parlour, and left him for a while.

As he waited for her return Finn again pondered on the goodness of this woman's heart. Not once had she derided him for being the idiot man that he was. What had he ever done to deserve the assistance of such a person? Once long ago, he and one of the gang members had gone into a church, mainly because it was pelting cats and dogs. The man up the front wearing a woman's dress, was going on about this God person who looked out for us. At the time Finn had wondered what he had ever done to be neglected by him. The man he had learnt was called a vicar had droned on, and in his boredom, Finn gazed about the church. When he asked his mate about the statues along the high walls of the place, he said he thought they were called angels. They all had their hands beneath their chins and his mate said they were likely praying to this God person. Once outside again he questioned his mate about these angel people and how he knew so much about them.

"Oh, they ain't people like us," his mate said. "They hang about up in some place in the sky and do good things I think."

"What sort of things?" Finn wondered.

"They sort of help people who are in trouble, so I was told," was his answer. "At one time some street woman told me all these things. She said she was something called a Catholic and the priest in her church once told her all this stuff."

Soon after, he and Esther went into a room set with small round tables. Finn had never tasted lamb so sweet as he tucked into a dinner served by another young wench. He felt quite like a member of the gentry as the other occupants of the room spoke to him and Esther pleasantly. Later, when Finn was comfortably settled in a room such as he had never had the pleasure of sleeping in before, as he lay on the comfortably soft bed, he told himself that Esther was like one of the angels and he was lucky enough to have met her. That thought worried him a bit, as he then worried that perhaps she was not of this world because she was so full of goodness.

What would he do if she went off up to that
place in the sky one day to join the angels,
and go help other people?

Chapter Ten

Esther plumped up her pillow when sleep evaded her. For so long it seemed she had waited for the time when she and Finn could be away from all the stresses the past weeks had brought upon them. Dare she mention marriage again, she wondered as she stared at the flickering candle on the small table beside the bed.

While waiting for him to arrive, she had wandered around this town and found it pleasant and a place she would like to put down roots. There was a hospital and a post office. One time she passed the small Anglican church and, on an impulse, went inside. A kindly vicar approached her and for a while they chatted idly. When she told him, "The man I intend to wed is joining me soon and I would very much like us to marry in your beautiful church. Would that be possible and what do I do to prepare for this event?"

The vicar went on in depth about the rules and when she left the church she wondered at her audacity. Would Finn still wish to go ahead with a marriage—or would he indeed ever arrive here? Could be he had felt her proposal just a stupid passing remark.

But now as she lay in the bed, she felt a sense of excitement along with anticipation. At least he had finally arrived with a good reason for being so late, so at least he did not have intentions of moving on elsewhere. Esther wished she knew more of how men thought about the world. Her Papa had talked at length about her finding a suitable marital partner to spend her life with and at the time she had surmised that most men were as honorable as he. A man such as Lawrence, so unlike Finn and her Pa in all ways, was simply looking for a wife with a fair dowry. She felt angry when she finally realised that due to Priscilla Clement's meddling, he had arrived with all intentions of marrying Esther to feather his nest.

Sleep finally claimed her, and as she dressed next morning a strange thrill caught her as she contemplated a life spent with Finn. He looked refreshed when he joined her in the dining room later. "How did you sleep?" she asked for something to say.

"Very well." Finn nodded to the man and his wife who sat at the adjoining table. "The bed was most comfortable." They spoke little as they enjoyed the breakfast of porridge followed by bacon slices, poached eggs, and freshly baked bread.

As they left the dining room, she said, "Finn, there is much we must discuss. Perhaps you could meet me down here and we can take a walk. It is a fair morning and I would like to show you around this sweet town." The inn overlooked the river and soon they found a bench where they could sit. She hesitated before saying, "I have gone over the few options I have of finding employment in this town. I considered teaching, so have to look into the chances of me doing that. I have a fair knowledge of all things medical due to my Papa's diligence, but sadly not enough to be able to earn a wage in that direction. And I certainly never gained any required certificates." She paused.

"I am so sorry about my stupidity, Esther. I am sure I could earn sufficient to keep you in your needs, but with this..." He lifted his bound arm. "I am useless at the moment."

Esther touched him gently on the knee. "No fear, Finn. Another of my ideas is for us to perhaps do something together." Again, she paused as she wondered how she dared continue.

"Together? But I know nothing of the things you speak of. No, I must do a man's work. All I know is how to saw logs and build a cage for the safety of chickens. And fight with my fists—and I am unsure if that will ever be possible now." He tapped his bound arm.

"Yes, I do understand that, but if I undertook a business that was in need of a man's strength as well as a woman's touch would that not be ideal? Of course, we would need to be wed to undertake such a future together." She could feel the heat rush to her cheeks at that outburst.

For a moment he seemed dumbfounded before saying, "I thought perhaps you were jesting when you made that suggestion before."

Unsure whether he himself was jesting with her, she said hastily, "I suppose at the time I was not thinking straight, but do you not think it an admirable plan? I would likely find it very difficult to even consider a business venture alone, but with a husband the bank, or for that matter anyone, would not hesitate to allow a legally bound pair to go into business." Esther really had no idea if that was true, for her Mama once told her of one or two well-known women who had quite successfully gone alone into ventures. Since coming to this town, she had learnt that the inn where they lodged was licensed in 1825 to a Mrs. Anne Bridger. And also, Esther had an inkling that it would likely be thought that at her age she should be considering matrimony and not commerce of any kind.

"Well, until I am of more use to you, I must simply follow whatever plans you make. But Esther, be sure that whatever you decide I would be honored to be a part of it."

Esther's smile was so wide that her jaws almost ached. "I took the liberty of speaking to the vicar at the church, and he has agreed to marry us. I explained our situation of both being without a family to back us up and he said we must find someone to vouch for us."

"Then who do you suggest?" Finn shook his head, looking totally befuddled at it all. Esther could see why he would be confused—she was confused enough herself at her boldness. "Of course, I know of nobody."

"Then let us find a man of the law and put our problem to him." Esther took Finn by the hand and together they went in search of a reputable notary.

And so, two days later they came from the church as man and wife. All done hastily with the assistance of Mr. Reginald Smithson, a tall forty something year old legal advisor with silver hair and a slight stutter in his speech. He had also insisted that should they need advice concerning a reputable business then they should be sure to seek him out.

Back at the inn they brought the innkeeper into their confidence and so late evening after a splendid dinner arranged by the inn's cook to celebrate the occasion, Esther uncertainly faced Finn in her room, now their shared bedroom. Yesterday Esther visited a nearby dressmaker's where the seamstress had provided her with a pretty nightdress of pink cotton with a frill around the high neck and also around each of the long sleeves. This she now wore, and realised belatedly that she should have also sought nightwear for him.

Finn looked a lot more nervous than she felt. He looked about the room as if, like a scared creature, he searched for somewhere to hide. "We can just go to sleep if that is what you wish, Esther," he said with a small shrug. "I realise that you are an innocent maiden and do not know the ways of men and their wants."

"You forget, I am the daughter of a surgeon who knew the intimacies of the human body. It is unfortunate that Papa left it to Mama to explain how we females produce babies, for she failed to tell me the entire story. She said she would go into detail about the marriage bed when I became betrothed to a man." Because Esther was certain her parents shared a great love for each other and knew that they shared a bed, she said tentatively, "Shall we just get into our bed, for I would dearly love to lie beside you, Finn. I do know that you most likely do not share a deep affection for me, so have no fear I will not be heartbroken whatever happens between us."

Saying nothing, he nodded and sat on the side of the bed to remove his boots, which she was pleased to see he arranged neatly beside each other. His jacket had already been hung on the hook behind the door, so once he had taken off his breeches and shirt, he waited until she was settled beneath the covers before climbing in beside her. He lay on his right side saying, "I fear I do not know what to do with this," as he faced her. The bandaged arm lay like a log on his chest.

"Just be as comfortable as you can," Esther said, hearing a small tremble in her voice. Now that he was so close, and scantily dressed in his undergarments, she could feel the heat coming from his body—his well-muscled body, and it sent a small quiver to her toes.

"I suggest you get some sleep as it has been a busy day or two." He turned onto his back. "Do you wish me to douse the candle?"

This was not turning out one tiny bit as Esther expected her wedding night would be—but on the other hand she really did not know what was expected of her. "Would you mind giving me a kiss goodnight first?" she asked, noticing a quiver of nervousness in the question. "I feel sure that is what we should do to seal the marriage pact." Having no idea if that was required anyway, she awkwardly turned and pressed her lips to his. He did not push her away but let her continue.

Esther knew that whatever happened next, she would forever remember just what it felt like to have his mouth pressed against hers. Despite his years of struggle and imprisonment his lips felt remarkably smooth and soft, and she could feel a tremble start at that point and then encompass her whole body. Even her toes clenched at the wonderful sensation.

His good arm went under and around her and he pulled her close. The kiss seemed to go on and on and when he gently pulled back, she lay down with a sigh. Thinking he would now bid her goodnight, a thrill ran through her when he asked, "Would it be all right if I now kiss you back, my wife?"

Without speaking Esther opened her arms to him. The second kiss was better by far, and without realising how it happened, Finn had raised her nightgown and his mouth was ever hotter as it went to first one breast and then the other. "You have a beautiful body," he whispered as he fondled her. "Oh, how I wish I had two good arms so that I could hold you closer."

Esther took that as an invitation and put her arms about him. "Then I will use both of mine to make up for your lack of one," she said, as without thinking any further she pressed even closer. Without knowing how it came about soon both of them were naked as newborn babes and what followed surprised and amazed her.

Esther awoke sometime later with a warm glow enclosing her whole body. Finn slept soundly at her side, and she studied his face by the light of the candle. His hair, as fair as any man's could be, was a tangle about his face—a face that she loved. When she thought more about it, she realised that this feeling she held for him must be of the kind her parents shared. At times she had caught a special look in their eyes when Papa had suggested they take to their beds early because he'd had a tiring day.

When Finn asked, "I did not hurt you, did I?" he surprised her, for she thought he still slept. With tenderness he stroked her side, setting her to trembling again.

"Oh no, I found it very pleasant." She suppressed a small laugh at that for it seemed a stupid thing to say at a time like this after what they had shared.

"That's good, for I should very much like to repeat it." He stopped stroking her and raised himself on his good elbow to look down at her. "You do realise that you will very likely bear a child after what we did, do you not?"

"To be honest, Finn, I should very much like to have a child—perhaps a son who looks like his Papa. That would be very nice. I think it is the expected thing when we are wed. My Mama told me once that she very much regretted only having the one daughter, for she believed that most men prefer a son to carry on their name."

"As I am unsure if my name is truly mine it matters not to me. All I wish is for you to be happy."

"Then happy I shall be, just as long as I have you by my side."

Only later did Esther realise that no words of love had been spoken. But his need for her to be happy must satisfy her. Two days later they went to see Reginald with their plea to find them a place to build their future together—preferably somewhere with a business attached, for they had to think of this future, especially if she now carried Finn's child, which she sincerely hoped she did.

"Leave it to me, dear people." Reginald hesitated while he looked down at a brown folder that he had in front of him on his desk. "Hmm, as it happens a business associate of mine put this opportunity to me only recently. How would you feel about a store that stocked most of their customers wants?"

Esther sat up straighter. "Why, that sounds perfect, Mister Smithson. In fact, it is just what I had in mind as it would suit us both. Especially if there is living quarters attached, for we really need to move from the hotel." Finn said nothing but nodded her way.

"Well then." Grinning widely, Reginald stood and came around his desk. "I will speak to this person and find out more and see when would be a suitable time for you to view the property." Esther noted that he seemed overjoyed at his idea.

Filled with excitement, she and Finn went along with Reginald the following morning which was a typical winter's day with steady rain from an overcast sky. The weather had produced cold, icy winds so Esther wore her new cape and gloves for warmth. As soon as Reginald opened the door of the store, she knew that this was just what she wanted. Glancing at Finn she was aware of his slight hesitation, so she whispered, "What do you think?"

"It matters not what I think, for you must decide, not me." Taking her by the arm he looped it through his good one.

The shelves of the store were packed with everything from fine woven fabrics to articles of clothing and the shelves on the other side were filled with foodstuffs. Reginald beckoned to a very thin man whose massive moustache curled up at each side over his cheeks. For some reason she could not understand, Esther felt a strange tingle up her spine, and it was not a pleasant tingle.

"This here is Mister Hammer, and he will show you around." Reginald flapped a hand as the man approached them.

"Good day to you." Mister Hammer's smile was barely visible beneath the huge whiskers on his face. An hour later Finn, as the husband, signed a paper stating their interest in purchasing and an agreement to hand over a bank cheque for the deposit of two hundred pounds within two days.

"Ideal decision," Reginald said after they left the store. He seemed to be rubbing his hands together in his satisfaction at a good deal done, but perhaps he felt the chill in the air. "If you would be so good as to pass the bank cheque to me as your legal representative, I will deal with all the documentation immediately so that you can take over the premises once the final sum is paid."

Over dinner back at the hotel, Finn said, "Are you quite certain you wish to go ahead with this, Esther? I have no sense of the right or wrong way of dealing with business matters, so it is entirely your choice. There is still time to back out of this. It is a huge responsibility—that is a very big store, and you probably have as little idea of running such a place as I have."

"I know, but Finn, I so want to be in charge of my life, and I love that the store sells just about everything needed in a household. I am sure we can learn the ins and outs of it in no time. We can keep the present staff on, and they seem capable." Esther placed her hand on his across the table. "Just think, we will be masters of our lives."

"Did you not think that Hammer cove seemed rather a shifty sort? His eyes kept going to Smithson as if he sought reassurance."

Esther had to admit such but kept that to herself for she so yearned for this to succeed. Later that night as they continued to become embroiled in their new-found passion, she forgot all else but her growing love for the man in her arms.

The bank manager seemed taken aback when they faced him with the news the next day. "Are you quite positive you wish to hand over such a large sum of money, Miss Blythe?" he asked.

"I am now Mrs. O'Connor," she told him pertly. "And this transaction is to bear my husband's name along with my own. We wish to have joint ownership of the store."

So, a few days later they packed their few belongings into the cart, harnessed Danny Boy to it and took off on their new adventure. Luckily there was a shed behind the store where Danny could be stabled at night, and also a very small yard for him to spend his days outside when the weather permitted. Esther was surprised that Reginald was not waiting on their arrival, and the staff seemed not to know anything about his whereabouts.

With great excitement Esther, along with Finn, introduced themselves to the staff of three. The man who appeared to be in charge seemed puzzled by their arrival and when Esther called him into the small room that served as an office behind the storeroom, he had no idea where Reginald Smithson, or indeed where the man Hammer was. It seemed they had not been notified of their arrival at all. The staff, in fact, seemed not to know much at all about the sale of the store. But that did not deter Esther, for she convinced herself that it was usual for the staff not to have information of such dealings.

Nevertheless, the staff were friendly and showed them around the store, briefly explaining the ordering system. A few customers came in and were served and left without speaking to Esther. Finn kept busy in the storeroom. Esther was proud of the way he seemed to adjust to what must have been an entirely new experience for him—having people around who looked up to him.

That evening when they retired to the small sitting room behind the store, after ensuring that Danny Boy got a good serving of grain when Finn settled him down in the small shed that would be his new home, Esther said, "Did you think it rather strange that Reginald Smithson did not make an appearance today? I thought he would at least be here to welcome us and ensure all was well."

Finn shook his head. "To be honest dear girl, I have been too astonished by the speed with which this has been accomplished, and really have no idea of its strangeness or otherwise."

The first fortnight of their new venture passed by in a blur of activity. Exactly fourteen days after taking up their positions as owners, Esther was in the storeroom with one of the female employees when a rather portly man burst open the door and demanded, "Just who do you think you are madam, and what are you doing in my store? I have no recollection of informing my staff of a new employee."

So dumbstruck was Esther that she simply stared at him. His jowls seemed to quiver and she presumed it was with anger for his face had also taken on a rosy hue. A minute or two went by before he shouted, "Well, speak up woman, you are not deaf and dumb, are you?"

An anger rose in Esther such as she had never known before as she neared him and demanded, "I think I should ask the same of you sir, just who do you think you are talking to?"

"Of that I have not the slightest idea. My dear wife and I are the co-owners of this establishment and left no orders before we went away a few weeks back for anyone to take on new staff in my absence."

"New staff?" Esther heard a note of something bordering on delirium in her tone as the enormity of this man's words hit home. The walls seemed to close in on her and she recalled nothing except a loud whooshing noise filling her head.

When she was revived by someone holding smelling salts beneath her nose, she was in the small parlour lying on the one sofa the room held. A woman who seemed as portly as the obnoxious man who had delivered the horrifying facts to her, was sitting beside her. Finn stood a foot or so away, a look of such dismay on his dear face she felt pity for him for being wed to such an idiot of a wife. He could take no blame whatsoever for this obvious travesty.

"I beg your forgiveness," the woman said in a lilting accent that Esther took to be either Scottish or Irish. "My husband was so shocked I fear he scared the life out of you, dear. How do you feel now?" She handed a small cup containing water to Esther and urged her to drink.

Esther shook her head as she looked up at Finn. "What did he say to you?" she asked.

"It seems that we have been hoodwinked by Reginald Smithson into buying a property that was not his to sell." Gently he helped the woman up and took her place beside Esther. "I have called the constable and he is right now out there talking to the real owner."

"Oh Finn, what have I made you do? I feel ashamed at my utter stupidity."

"Don't worry. I have faced worse disasters in my life. The constable will sort it out, do not fear." He stroked her hand and pushed her hair that had come loose from its chignon back over her shoulder. Esther wasn't so certain and by the look on Finn's face he only half believed his words that were surely meant to comfort her.

Esther's mind was in such a confused
jumble that she was only half aware of the
constable's questions that seemed to go on
forever.

Chapter Eleven

Finn paced the room. They had relocated back to the hotel until the whole mess could be sorted out—if it ever would be. His anxiety for Esther grew with each day, for her state of health did not seem to improve, instead got worse as she fretted about what they would do next. Fortunately, she had not depleted her entire funds on the awful blunder, so they could stay here for now, but sooner rather than later they would have to decide on where to go next. Sadness filled him that her cherished dream had been a fantasy, and he feared she would wither and die if she did not snap from this mood of despair.

"Finn, I have an idea." Her voice brought him out of his dour mood, for she sounded as if she was almost back to her normal self. He went to sit on the bed beside her. She pulled her shawl around her shoulders as she sat up. "Perhaps I can find employment with a family as I did before, and care for their children."

Much as Finn thought that idea was not a good outcome, at least it proved that she was thinking ahead. "If that is what you would like to do then do it. I can always find work somewhere. As a matter of fact, I was talking to a man in the nearby public house." When that news seemed to upset her, he stroked her cheek. "Now don't get worried, I was told by the owner of the inn that it was the best place for me to find employment."

"Oh, perhaps he is right. And did you meet anyone who might be in need of a handyman?"

"No, but I did talk to the owner of what is apparently a thriving company that deals in imported stock. When I told him that my wife owned a small wagon he was interested—said I could go back and forth between here and Hobart transporting his smaller wares that come in steamships from Sydney Town and elsewhere in the colonies. What do you think?"

She looked slightly doubtful as she thought this prospect over, but then said, "Well, it would be good for Danny as he does not like being idle, and also good for you to have something to do rather than watch over me."

About to tell her that would never be a problem for him, Finn kept quiet. At least he would be earning an honest living. "I also met another man who was talking about a small cottage he owned that his mother had lived in. It seems that she has gone to live with her daughter, and instead of selling the place he would prefer to let it out for the time being if he could find suitable tenants who would take care of it."

She seemed to brighten at that piece of news. "That sounds a good prospect, Finn, for we cannot stay here indefinitely. Do you know where to get in touch with this man again?"

He did, and so it worked out that as October came in and the spring weather brightened, they were settled into the cottage. It was close to the river and had a small lean-to at the rear where Danny Boy could keep out of the worst weather with room at its side to keep the cart. Finn made his first successful trip to Hobart for which he received payment. The only downside was that he was away from Esther for one night. The furnishings in the cottage were old and threadbare as was to be expected of an older lady who had lived alone for some time, but at least Esther appeared to be happy to spend the day cleaning and doing her best to brighten the surroundings.

"The constable called while you were not here," she said on his return. "He seems to think that the man and his wife who said they were the owners of the store were an untrustworthy pair who might in some way share an alliance with Reginald Smithson and the despicable Hammer person."

Astounded at that piece of news, Finn rubbed his brow. "So, does he then expect you to recoup some of your losses?"

She looked doubtful. "He has to find proof, but at least he is doing his best for us. Without substantial proof it is just a matter of waiting to see what eventuates."

Finn had many doubts about the constable doing his best. His distrust of those in charge had not totally disappeared during his time of freedom. For all he and Esther knew, the constable could be in with them also.

When Finn returned from his second trip to Hobart, Esther met him while he was removing Danny's harness. After giving him a welcome kiss and giving Danny a pat, she said, "I have found employment. I visited our landlord to pay our rental, and he happened to mention during our conversation how his poor wife was worn out looking after her three small children. I questioned him on their ages, and it seems she gave birth to a daughter a few months back. One boy is about three and the eldest nearer six. I explained that I had formerly been a companion and nanny without mentioning who for and I would very much like to do that again.”

“Are you certain of this, Esther, for there is no need of you working now that I can earn a regular wage.”

With a shake of the head, she said, “But I am not the sort of person who can simply spend her days pottering about Finn, I must do something of interest to keep me busy.” As they walked into the kitchen, she asked, “So how was your journey this time? Are you certain that you enjoy doing this Finn?”

Truth was he hated being away from her for even a minute, but said, “My boss is pleased with me, but I will not lie and say it is pleasurable. He has mentioned that he now wants me to drive his sturdier wagon because he wishes to move larger merchandise—he is expanding his business into selling furniture and other household needs.”

As he had expected, Esther did not look pleased with that news. “But Danny Boy is not up to pulling a larger load. That would require at least two horses.”

Finn took her hand in his. “Have no fear, he already owns two wagons and I would be using two of his horses. I think it will be easier for me as I can then likely do the trip in one day so therefore would not be away from you overnight.”

"Ah, that is surely a good plan, for I can then use Danny to take me to my new place of employment which is over the far side of the town. I miss taking my boy for drives, and I hate it when you are not here with me at night."

"So, all is well. Come now, let me hold you and tell you how much I missed you while away." Finn pulled her close.

When Finn came home after his next uneventful trip to Hobart, Esther came running with the news that the constable had called in with exciting news. "The troopers caught up with Reginald Smithson on his way up north with his good lady wife. It seems we were not the only ones he deceived. Another man was duped into handing over his well-earned savings."

"And will you be receiving at least part of your lost money?"

"Sadly, they are still in the process of trying to uncover just where he has deposited it. The constable assured me that they are doing their best. Currently Smithson is awaiting trial in Hobart jail. It may take months for us to hear good news. Hammer, his accomplice, has disappeared. For all we know he is now on a ship sailing far away from here."

As the Christmas of eighteen forty-eight neared, they had still not heard anything of the lost money. Smithson was now in Port Arthur prison for which seemed to Finn to be a just and fair sentence of ten years. Esther was expecting a child which was due to be born—or so she thought—sometime the following April or May. So far, her small bump did not seem to interfere with her looking after the Grace's offspring. She seemed to be enjoying her task of trying to teach the boys of about four and six their letters and numbers.

"Are Mr. and Mrs. Grace aware that you will be unable to carry on tending to their children as the birth time nears?" Finn asked as they sat on the sofa after their evening meal. "And you most certainly will not be able to drive the cart then." He stroked her belly fondly.

"Oh yes, Mrs. Grace asked me only yesterday when we expected the baby to be born. I told her that my problem as my size increases will be climbing aboard the cart, so I would be unable to continue much longer. I do so enjoy caring for their offspring. The two boys are scamps, but lovable." She sighed. "I long for this baby of ours to be out of me, Finn. You are excited, aren't you?"

"Of course, my love. Only a year ago I would never have dreamed of being married to a sweet girl like you, let alone be looking forward to our first child."

Next morning Finn kissed Esther one more time and strode off. He now picked up the larger wagon and horses from the stables behind the property of his employer. A hot wind blew in from the sea as he started out with the empty wagon. The road was becoming very familiar to him now and he whistled as he went along. The two horses were larger than Danny Boy and certainly had little trouble pulling what was now regularly a heavy load.

His load this time consisted of a few small pieces of furniture picked up from the factory where they had been fashioned and a chest that the owner told Finn to take extra care of, but did not go on to explain what its contents were. Accustomed by now to carrying many unusual pieces of cargo he did not question the man, but set off in the hope of reaching home before the sun began to sink.

On reaching about the halfway point, he spotted a group of riders that seemed to be loitering at the side of the road. The daily coach had passed him a while back and there were no other vehicles in front of him or behind. Guessing the men were simply taking a break from their journey, it surprised him when one rider moved his mount across the road, blocking it. As he slowed the horses, he was surprised even more when he recognised the rider as Bear, the brute who had gained his hatred while at the penitentiary and later.

"Well, well, if it ain't old Finn the Irish no-hoper," he shouted as Finn stopped a short distance in front of his mount. "Done all right for yerself 'ave yer?" Taking off his hat he wiped at his not too clean face, before giving what Finn took as a signal to his five co-riders who moved forward to join him.

"So, Bear, did you escape or don't tell me you were actually let out," Finn said with a false bravado while he had a feeling this crowd were not out to just pass the time of day with him.

Waving his hat before plonking it back on his head, Bear chuckled before saying, "The old Bear here was set free—done me time same as you didn't I? Meet me mates here." He gestured to his bunch of fellow riders.

"Would you mind telling your mates to move off the road then, so that I can pass." For the first time since taking on this job, a touch of what he took to be fear crawled up his spine. He suspected Bear was likely lying, as he had a vague remembrance that his term was not up for another five or so years. His crime had been murder, which he'd sworn was a lie—said the bloke started the fight that ended in his death.

"What you got in yer wagon then?" Bear took no heed of Finn's demand and grinned slyly.

"Just a bunch of old furniture—nothing that would be of interest to you, Bear." Making the decision to try and bypass the men, Finn clicked his tongue and used his whip to encourage the horses to move forward. Bear was too quick though, and forestalled him by gripping the reins of the horse nearest to him. The animal tossed its head to no avail, while Bear signaled to one of his mates who grabbed the reins of the other horse.

"Take a look, Ernie," Bear shouted and a weedy looking fellow with a massive filthy beard almost reaching his belly, dismounted, handed his reins to one of the others and came across to peer into the rear of the wagon. Most of the load was covered for protection of the forecast rain, so as Ernie tried to whip the covers off, Finn saw his chance of escape. He brought the whip up and with an almighty shout urged the horses forward.

The one that Bear held reared and squealed and almost knocked Bear from the saddle, causing the other horse to panic and it too reared before both took off at a fast pace. Not sure what happened next as Finn was too busy trying to keep the pair steady as they began to race forward, he heard the man Ernie cursing and screaming as, legs flailing, he fell to the ground.

With a shouted string of vile curses Bear ordered the other four to give chase. One of them reached level with the bench where Finn sat and dragged at the reins in Finn's hands, pulling him sideways. The horses slowed as Finn fell, just missing the front wheels of the wagon as he dropped to the ground. Dirt filled his mouth as he opened it to yell before the sensation of falling was followed by blackness.

When Finn opened his eyes, a stranger was kneeling at his side shaking his shoulders and urging him to wake up. "Wha...what happened, where am I?" he mumbled.

"You're at the side of the road, matey, but not sure how you got here. Can you recall how you came to be lying here?" The man had a pleasant face, its many lines proving that he had spent hours out in the sun and wind. "Can you get up? That's a mighty wound you have on you, chum. Looks like you fell off your horse. Did it gallop off and leave you here?"

Feeling as if he had fallen off a cliff, and drifted where the world was whirling about him, Finn struggled to a sitting position and wiped at the blood streaming down from a cut on his forehead. "Can't remember," he mumbled, looking about to see if a stray horse was nearby. The only animal, which he guessed belonged to this bloke, was now pulling at the grass along the side of the road. "Think I fell but not sure how. You didn't see my horse, did you?"

"Nah. I was just passing on my way home." The stranger took off his hat, scratched at his head and looked about before putting it back on his head. "Hope to get back before sundown. I suppose you were on the way home, eh?"

Finn shook his head, now throbbing with pain. "Can't say I know." Giving it a think over he had a sudden recollection of being on a wagon but had no idea where that could have come from. "You didn't happen to see a wagon of some sort, did you?"

"Nah. Look, mate, how about you come along with me? My old nag can carry two. I guess you must be from New Norfolk, eh? If nothing comes back to you along the way, I'll drop you off at the police shop and let them work out where you belong. Perhaps your horse will be grazing along the way somewhere."

"Thank you, that's kind of you." The name of the town sounded vaguely familiar, so Finn thought it was as good a place as any to go. No point in staying out here when nighttime fell.

The man whistled and his horse came over to him. He mounted, gave Finn a hand up behind him and the horse began to amble along at the road's edge. A couple of other riders passed them at a fair pace, waving a greeting before continuing on. Finn racked his brain in an effort to recall how he came to be on the ground out here miles from anywhere, with no luck. The only memory was the brief flash of a wagon. Tormented by the feeling that he should be somewhere or with someone, plus the pain in his head, made him feel dizzy.

Because the horse did not break from his slow amble, night was falling as they passed a few cottages of what Finn guessed was the town they were heading towards. The pain in his head worsened while he tried to search for something familiar in the surroundings.

"Not sure if I should take you to the constable or the hospital," his rescuer said. "Perhaps might be best to let the constable decide what to do with you." Soon he pulled his horse up in front of what Finn presumed was where they would find the constable this man kept referring to. "Down you get, mate." Finn slid off the horse awkwardly, feeling dizzier than ever, ending up sitting on the path in front of the building. "I'll just explain how I came across you."

Hooking his reins over a post in front of the building, he left Finn sitting there before going to the door. "Thank you," Finn called out, and the kind fellow doffed his hat before striding off. It occurred to Finn then that he had not asked the stranger his name.

Some time went by and Finn must have dozed for someone shook his arm, saying, "The chief here reckons he knows you." Finn was sure he had never set eyes on the man he gestured to.

Coming to stand over Finn, he asked, "So, young fellow, what happened to get you in this state?" Without waiting for a response, he continued, "That is one nasty cut you have there on your head. This man here will escort you home."

Shaking his head Finn asked, "How is it you know where my home is?"

"Well now, that's a long story. Might be best if you let your wife tell you that."

"My wife?" Finn felt as if he was floating around in a sea of mud. He had a wife! "Would you mind telling me my name in that case, sir. And the name of this wife you say I have."

"Dear me, seems like you have a bad case of what the doc calls concussion, young fellow. Your name is Finn O'Connor and your wife is Esther. Nice young woman who let herself get hoodwinked by a clever thief. Anyway, best let her explain the rest to you.

Doc also says that the memory returns in perhaps a day or two, so then you won't feel so confused."

Confused didn't half cover Finn's feelings as he walked along the street beside the young police officer. He racked his brain to try and make sense of this whole thing, making his head ache even more. "Do you happen to know what your chief meant when he said my wife was hoodwinked?" he asked.

"Not really sure. Something to do with the sale of property, I think. They caught the bloke who was to blame. I know he's now locked up."

That short explanation only made Finn more confused. "Locked up where?" he asked, feeling like a four-year-old short of brains.

"Good heavens, you are in a bad way if you don't know about the penitentiary at Port Arthur." Stopping beside a cottage where a lamp burned behind the blind, he said, "Well, this is where your wife will no doubt be awaiting you." Without another word he turned and retraced his steps.

Finn watched him walk away and then went to the door and tapped lightly on it. No sense of homecoming hit him, and he wondered if perhaps they had the wrong man and the police chief had confused him with someone else. The door opened just enough for him to see a woman the other side. When she saw him there, she threw the door wide and pulled him into her arms crying, "Finn, where have you been? I was worried half out of my mind. Your employer called in some time ago asking if you had returned from your trip to Hobart. It seems you were expected hours ago."

The woman smelt of lavender and some other scent that he found familiar but for the life of him could not fathom what it was. She was the most beautiful woman he had ever seen, and his tongue stuck to the roof of his mouth as he wondered what to tell her.

"You are hurt. Oh, Finn, come inside and let me tend to your wound. What happened?" Catching him by the arm, she ushered him into the room. It was by no means a luxurious dwelling with furniture that looked as if it had been around for many years. He had been hoping that once he saw the woman and his place of residence, some memory would return, but nothing sprang to mind.

After rummaging about in a drawer of the simple dresser, she produced some rags and then went to pour water from the kettle sitting atop the stove into a bowl. She then poured more cold water straight from the tap above the sink and came back. While she dabbed at the cut, he tried not to wince and asked, "How long have I been missing?"

That seemed to surprise her. Looking at the old clock sitting atop the mantelpiece over the fireplace she said, "Hours. As you see it is past two o clock and you are always home before tennish."

Feeling that it was time to tell her the truth he blurted, "I fear I cannot remember," sounding again like a small child.

"You mean you have lost your memory once again. Oh Finn." She dabbed at his face some more and then rinsed the blood-soaked rag in the small bowl.

"Again?" He stared at her. "Do I make a habit of getting bashed on the head then?"

After gently spreading some salve onto the gash, she said, "As it happens, you did have a nasty fall when you broke your arm some time ago and did forget things for a short period. My Papa told me once that a knock to the head often leads to loss of memory."

A strange feeling went up one arm and he looked down at it, puzzled. "Your Papa? Is he a doctor then?"

His question seemed to perplex her and for a moment she simply stared at him. "My dear Finn, I think the best thing for now is for you to lie down, and tomorrow we will learn exactly what befell you to put you in this state of mind." Going to the drawer

again, she brought a strip of rag over and
after binding his head with it said, "Come, I
will show you where the outhouse is and
then we will get some sleep."

Chapter Twelve

Esther watched Finn sleep. What on earth had befallen him this time to be in such a state of confusion? Softly she stroked his brow when he muttered a few words she could not understand. Settling down beside him she stared at the ceiling, and eventually she must have dozed for a loud banging brought her out of a strange dream where she and Finn had been lost in a forest.

The banging woke Finn too and he sat up, staring about the room as if trying to fathom where he was. "What's that?" he cried as he turned to put his feet to the floor.

"Someone is at our door, and it seems they are impatient." Leaning across she patted his arm. "Stay here and I will see who it is." As she pulled her shawl about her shoulders she asked, "Do you recall where you are Finn?"

With a shake of the head he said, "No, what am I doing here?"

She went out before he rose from the bed and closed the door after her. As she opened the door a stranger barged past her, yelling, "Where is the cove who lost my possessions?"

Guessing it must be Finn's employer she said as gently as she could, for his face was so set in a fierce scowl that she feared he was fit to kill, "Finn was attacked I think, for he has been severely bashed and is suffering from concussion."

"Concussion!" She expected steam to come from his ears as he exploded the word. "I'll give him concussion—the stupid bastard. He's lost my fine horses and wagon, not to mention some valuable possessions."

"Oh, I am sorry for your loss, Mister..." Realising she had no idea of his name she said, "Er, Sir, Finn was brought back by a kind person who found him at the side of the road, and delivered him to the police office."

"I heard all this from them, but I wish to hear from the idiot himself." Legs astride he scowled around the room. "Fetch him if you will."

Anger swelled in Esther. "My husband is no idiot, sir. And if I might suggest something, if your load was so valuable then should not Finn be accompanied by a trooper on the road or at least another driver?"

Whether that question was ever to be answered she did not know for Finn then appeared at the door. The man faced him and shook his fist in his direction shouting, "Thank the lord my horses were found not far from their stable, my man. It seems the thieves were not interested in any of the other contents of the wagon but made off with the chest you carried."

"The chest?" Finn's brow wrinkled as if he tried his best to understand what this man was saying. Confirming his ignorance of the matter, he added, "What chest is that?"

"As you see my husband cannot remember any of the day's events." Esther lifted her chin. "He has a nasty wound on his head so must have been badly attacked, likely by a gang of thieves."

"Bear." Both Esther and the man turned as Finn blurted the one word.

"Don't be daft, we don't have bears in this part of the world." Bringing a fisted hand up towards Finn's face he threatened, "I'll have you sent to the asylum if you keep this up, laddie."

Fear curled inside Esther then. She turned beseeching eyes to Finn and asked gently, "Was that the name of the man who attacked you, Finn?"

With a swift nod, he said, "Yes, I remember I didn't like him a lot and he is large. He had some mates along with him. I think I knew him from somewhere but can't be sure."

"Oh right, here he goes again with his silly notions. Time to tell the truth now. Perhaps you did know him and perhaps you were in with this Bear cove, eh? That sounds more like a touch of the truth."

The fear grew stronger in Esther as she imagined this man accusing Finn in a court of law of assisting with the robbery. He was certainly capable of getting Finn sent to prison for that, and it would be doubtful if Finn could stand that suffering again. "No, no," she screamed. "Finn would never be an accomplice to criminals. He is an honest man. Has he not fulfilled his duties to you up until this incident? Now, have you been to the constable with your story? Finn was taken there and has given his side of the events that occurred." She was not sure if that was totally true but guessed it was.

"Of course, I have. I'm not the guilty one here, I had my property stolen because of your husband's stupidity." He shook a fist Finn's way.

"I suggest you take it up with the police now, for Finn can do no more." Glancing at Finn she saw by his frown that he was likely trying his hardest to recollect what really happened.

"Do no more." His shout went through her head that already ached with his yelling. "He obviously knows the name of the bloke who led the gang."

"Ah, so you admit it was a gang. Why don't we just now wait until it is sorted out by the constable. My husband will go there as soon as he is fit and explain that he thinks he knows the name of the gang leader who committed this robbery."

"I admit to nothing, madam. But I will head over to find out what the police know." With that, he stomped to the door, opened it, and slammed it shut on going out.

Finn slumped into a chair, head in hands. "I am so sorry," he said on a sob. "I do think I know the name of the man who was the gang leader. That much is coming back to me. I was going about my normal duty." He stopped and looked up at Esther. "Was I on the road back from Hobart?"

"Yes, yes. You had been there to pick up a load from the furniture manufacturers and you are usually home soon after dusk. I was so worried when you did not arrive and did not know what to do. I waited an hour or so and then went to the police office to enquire if they had heard anything of an accident along the road."

"Do I do this journey often?" he asked.

"Sometimes twice a week. Your employer has another driver I believe." A sudden thought hit Esther and she asked, "He pays you after each trip you make, does he not?" When he shook his head as if the question puzzled him, she added, "So that means that he will not be keeping his promise this time although he has recovered most of his load. I wonder what was in the chest that was so important. You don't recall, do you?"

"Sorry, I think that I probably had to just load it onto the wagon and deliver it."

"No sense in worrying ourselves further, Finn. Let us have breakfast and perhaps more will come to you as the day goes on."

Sadly, it did not. They ate breakfast and later lunch and still all Finn could remember was that someone he was sure was called Bear held him up, knocked him from the wagon and left him lying there. As they lay side by side in bed that night, Esther said, "Tomorrow I must go to my place of employment. I will tell the people I work for that I am unable to attend to my duties for a while and I will wait until you feel more like yourself before I continue there."

"You have to work?" he asked, seeming to be surprised. "Do I not provide us with enough to pay our way?"

Esther felt the need to explain to him in detail what had occurred that led them to take on employment. She did not tell him that he was an ex-convict, feeling that he had enough to contemplate at the moment.

In the middle of the night, she awoke to see him sitting on the side of the bed with his head in his hands. Touching his back she asked, "What worries you, Finn?"

"Everything." She felt certain that he had been weeping, for his voice had a croak in it. "I am a useless husband it seems."

"No, you are not." She went onto her knees behind him and put her arms about him. "You are the best husband you can be, and I love you dearly, Finn." As she said the words, Esther realised that it was probably the one and only time she had actually told him of her true feelings.

"How can you possibly love a man who cannot even provide a decent living for you? A man who is stupid enough to get himself into this trouble? Now I am without employment if that man is to be believed, and you have to go out to support us both."

"Come now, lie beside me, dearest, and we will continue this discussion when your memory is back to normal."

He did this, but although she slept fitfully for the remainder of the night, she feared he did not. When he did doze, he was tormented, if his mutterings could be a sign of his anguished thoughts.

Esther awoke as the sun slanted across the bed, which was empty. Guessing that Finn was likely in the kitchen, she quickly dressed. The kitchen was empty, so thinking him to be outside she hastily poured water into the basin in the sink and washed her hands and face. By the time she had finished drying herself there was still no sign of him. Needing to use the outhouse she went out to the small garden. Danny Boy was busily munching on his grain, so it was obvious that Finn had given him his morning feed. Patting Danny's head she asked, "Where's Finn?" With a shake of the head, the h-+orse seemed to tell her he did not know.

Puzzled, she called Finn's name and got no answer, so began to worry that he might have wandered off while still not knowing who he was or what had passed yesterday. She went back inside and then caught sight of a sheet of paper lying on the shelf of the dresser. It was tucked beneath the small vase that Finn had presented her with after one of his trips to Hobart. As she picked it up and saw the first line of the words written on the page, the vase slipped out of her hands and smashed as it crashed onto the stone floor.

Finn had always fretted that he had never learnt to read and write as well as her.

Since their meeting she had assisted him with his letters, and he was proud of his progress. Esther slumped onto a chair by the table and her fingers shook as she began to read. Some of the words were misspelt and some jumbled but what he said was that he had recalled who he was, and what had occurred on the road. He thought that he was ignorant scum, that she deserved better, and he was unworthy of her love, and so was going back to where he knew he belonged, with his own kind of people. Tears dripped onto the page. She lay it down on the table as she wiped at her cheeks with the hem of her skirt. "Oh Finn," she moaned as she rocked back and forth. "What have you done? I need you now. How could you do this to me?"

Resting her face in her hands on the table she let the tears fall unheeded and sobbed until her throat was sore and her eyes blurred. A small glimmer of hope rose as she thought perhaps he might have second thoughts and return once he realised how foolish this was. Realising that it was Monday and she still had her commitments with the Grace children she sighed, and rose to put the kettle on. After brewing a pot of tea, she sat at the table again and reread the note. By people of his own kind, she could only surmise that he was returning to the dock area of Hobart where he would either meet up with men like Scottish Macduff, and thus end up using his fists again, or return to a brothel in search of work.

Both ideas made her feel sick, and she retched over the sink until her insides hurt. The baby kicked, reminding her that she owed it to the child to keep her sanity and good health, so she prepared toast and spread it with butter and her favourite plum jam. Unfortunately, after one mouthful she retched again. Losing all track of time as she walked about as if in a daze, she decided it best if she went to the Grace home as usual. Scribbling a note of explanation just in case Finn had a change of mind and returned, she went out and with great difficulty harnessed Danny Boy to the cart. Wondering if she should first go to the police to let the constable know what had happened, she decided against it.

Matilda Grace was kinder than her husband, who could be gruff and distant, and once Esther explained her tardiness to her, she said, "My dear girl, do not worry yourself. I suggest you stay here overnight. You say you left your husband a note, so he will know where you are should he arrive home to the empty house."

Relief filled Esther for once again a fear of loneliness made her feel faint. For a short time, living with Finn with the thought that soon they would be turning into the family she had always yearned for, she felt such happiness. This joyous feeling had disappeared. If Finn never returned to share her life, she would be bringing a child up alone, and the thought of this made her feel faint with sorrow. Matilda Grace along with her children made her feel almost as if she was a part of a real family. Mr. Grace was seldom home anyway, so it was left to his wife Matilda to run the household—a task she did remarkably well.

"My Mama was a strict and law-abiding person who taught me how to treat my staff," she told Esther once, and Esther had learnt that as an employer she was fair and just. The eldest boy George was inclined to be wayward and naughty, but soon would be the responsibility of a tutor who had been hired by his Papa. Esther had grown to love four-year-old Carmicheal, and the baby girl, Jemima.

Esther stayed in their household overnight. Well, she went to bed in their guest room, but sleep evaded her. Realising that all her tossing and turning was not good for her unborn child she tried to sleep but only managed a short nap or two. "You can stay here as long as you want to, my dear," Matilda assured her at the end of that day when Esther prepared to leave. "So, if your husband has not returned, I suggest you pack a few of your belongings and prepare for a longer stay—think of it as a holiday."

Unable to even consider it such a treat, nevertheless Esther was so grateful she shed more tears. A small glimmer of hope rose in her as she opened the door to the cottage and called his name. It soon faded when she knew for sure that there was no presence of Finn. He had even taken a bag with him and some articles of clothing. After another night of tossing and turning she felt drained of all energy as she took Matilda Grace's advice and pushed a few changes of clothing plus her hairbrush into a valise. After forcing herself to eat a small amount of porridge, she took a deep breath and went out to harness Danny.

Fortunately, Mr. Grace employed a stable boy to care for his two horses so Danny was taken care of by him and would spend his days alongside their horses in a small yard and his nights in the stables. The two older Grace children were in a frenzy of excitement when she went into the kitchen. Esther soon found this was caused by the oncoming festive season which had completely left her mind. This took her thoughts from her own troubles for a short time as she helped them with their childish decorations and gift wrapping.

After three more sleepless nights she not only felt weary but was endlessly sickly. "That is to be expected, my dear," Matilda said on noticing her plight. "During my period of expecting the birth of Jemima, I was also very sick and poorly."

Esther was thankful she worked in the household of such a thoughtful person. Memories of Mona Franklin and Priscilla Clements sprang to mind, and she doubted if either of them would have spared a moment's sympathy for her plight. Mr. Grace often seemed quite unaware that Esther was now living there, or if he was aware he paid her scant attention. In fact, he treated his wife as if she was of no importance. This only made Esther miss Finn more, for she was sure he was a better husband to her, and would be a better father to this child she carried. Each night she sent up a prayer for his safety. Even though her parents had never stressed the importance of religion of any kind in their household, she took comfort from the feeling that some power beyond her comprehension might be hearing these pleas.

Glad once the festive season was over, she now began to feel nervous, for she had no idea when her child would come into the world. "How will I know when my baby is to be born?" she asked Matilda on the first day of the New Year.

"Ah, did your Mama never explain childbirth to you?" Matilda seemed puzzled by this lack of information in Esther's upbringing. This made Esther feel that perhaps her Mama had been rather careless, for she had not ever gone into the subject of what being married entailed, let alone to explain how babies were created. Only by reading periodicals on medical procedures had she learnt a few facts after their wedding. This made her more miserable as she now missed her Mama as well as her departed husband, feeling as if there might be some fault in herself.

"My Mama was killed before she ever got around to explaining such details," she said feeling that by saying such she was now casting blame on her dear Mama.

"Do you have some idea when the baby was conceived, dear girl?" Matilda pulled Esther gently down beside her on the sofa.

Nibbling her lip, she hesitated before saying, "I think perhaps that happened soon after our marriage which took place at the beginning of August." She could not be sure if that was true either, but with her scant knowledge guessed it must be right.

"Your belly is not too large, but then again you are very slenderly built. A pregnancy takes about nine months, so I suggest your child will arrive late April or perhaps May. I will send for my physician, and he will be able to give you more information." Saying that she patted Esther's hand and rose to go about her business. The boys had already become aware of her changing shape and only yesterday George had told her that she must have eaten too much dinner.

As it happened the physician, a burly man with a brusque manner, repeated almost the same estimate as Matilda on when to expect the child, so she thought perhaps he had no more idea of the true date than she had herself. He did tell her what to expect though, and then had a conversation with Matilda on contacting the midwife who attended at the birth of her children, when the time came.

Often Esther felt more like Matilda's sister or daughter than a member of her staff. It made life somewhat easier to know that she was being treated as such rather than as a nanny or nurse. Often Esther felt that her employer was glad to have someone to confide in. But Matilda also showed a real interest in her cook and the young maid who did the household chores, as well as the stableboy who took care of the garden and the horses. Esther presumed that she was content with her life, even though her husband bestowed her and anyone else scant attention.

The weeks flew by as Esther neared her expected birthing date and she awoke towards the end of April knowing that what the doctor advised would happen had indeed happened, as water poured from her uncontrollably. Thinking at first that she simply had need of the chamber pot, fluid gushed out. Esther called out and the young maid who happened to be going about her morning duties and was outside Esther's door, came running in. She along with the cook had been warned of what would be happening to Esther. "I'll call madam," she cried as she rushed out again.

The midwife was there within the hour and Esther's daughter came into the world about four hours later. "You are so lucky," Matilda said after the midwife had completed her duties. "I was almost a day and a night producing my first child. What will you call her?"

Esther had already planned that if she gave birth to a son, it would be called Finlay or a daughter to be called Fern which she felt was most similar to Finn. She shed a few tears once left alone with her baby, whispering, "If only your Papa were here, he would be so proud and happy, my child." If only she knew where he was, Esther felt sure that if news got to him of the birth of his child, he would return post haste. Not a day or night since he left went by without her pondering on his whereabouts, and that night she told herself and her daughter that she would go and seek him out the moment she was able.

Chapter Thirteen

"Come on you lazy bugger, shift yerself." Finn felt a jab to his chest, but didn't open his eyes at the command. The crowd that had gathered to watch this latest fist fight were all yelling and screaming abuse, but he decided to lay where he had dropped and just ignore them all.

The usual pain in his shoulder and arm that came with being used as a punch bag was there as it always was after taking a beating. Not that he was often on the receiving end of the punches, but this time he seemed to have lost all enthusiasm for this game. Macduff was not overly concerned anyway, for at times he preferred Finn to drop as he backed the other idiot and came into a tidy sum. Finn usually did all right too. Macduff had convinced him that it paid to lose sometimes.

That suited him for he saw himself as a complete loser. Once all memory returned, he considered Esther would be better off by far without him hanging around. With difficulty he allowed himself to be hauled to his feet and he walked off amid the boos and abusive shouts of those in the hall who must have lost their weekly earnings. More fool them, he thought to himself. Most probably had women at home awaiting their return. It still puzzled him to this day just why Esther had seen fit to take a fool such as he along with her.

Yes, she would likely have her life sorted out by now and was happily living without him. A small niggle of shame bit at him when he thought of their unborn child. No doubt she had already brought a son or a daughter into the world—and probably done it ably without him. Nevertheless, his heart ached when he thought of the child growing up without him. At least he would have a sensible and caring Ma, unlike Finn who had never known such pleasures.

As Finn pulled on his breeches and shirt, Macduff came up to him and pressed some notes into his palm. "Here you go, my boy," he said with a sly grin. "Be ready on Saturday for the next bout." He leaned closer to mutter, "This one you must win. They will all be betting against you after tonight's loss so we will be laughing heartily." He strode off, probably to go to the public house to arrange how he would make his next windfall.

Finn had other ideas. As he lay on the dirt floor in agony, he told himself this would be the final time he would use his fists in a brawl or his body for the pleasure of the onlookers. Problem was, he had little idea what else to do. During the bout he had spotted a familiar little figure in the crowd, so once fully dressed he went in search of Paddy. The dwarf was nowhere to be seen, so Finn left the hall and walked along the street, heading for the brothel owned by Vera. As he neared the familiar house, he saw Paddy chatting to a couple of men, so stood nearby until they walked off and called, "Hey Paddy, thought I saw you back there. How's life at Vera's establishment?"

Paddy appeared to be puzzled for a moment, but must have then recognised Finn for he hailed him. "Well, well, is that you, Finn? Not a good outcome this night—lost good money on you I did. That Macduff up to his old shenanigans, is he?"

Without answering that question, for Paddy knew the answer as well as he did, he asked, "You still working for her?" He jabbed an arm in the general direction of the brothel.

"Nah, didn't you hear, she went off with one of her rich regulars a while back. As it happens, I kept the shop open and the girls are all happy to work for me. Vera handed the keys to little old Paddy." He patted his chest.

Finn's head went back in shock. "Well, that's a turn up for the books. They all the same ladies?"

"Sure are. One happy little family, that's us. The late-night crowd will be heading along soon, so I'd best get off." Paddy wrinkled his brow as if in thought. "Matter of fact we are doing so well I am thinking of taking on another knockabout. You know what the customers are like."

Finn did and remembered well the worst one of all. "Did you get any more trouble from that Lawrence bloke?"

"Nah, last I heard he had returned across the seas. Good riddance, I say. Anyhow, I have a thought, how about coming to work for me then? Must be better than getting used for punching practice, mate." Paddy began to walk away after beckoning to Finn. "Come in and say hello to the ladies anyway. Think a couple of them had a soft spot for you."

Of all the odd people Finn had worked for since becoming a free man, he was sure Paddy was likely better by far than the lot of them. Working in the brothel was not his first choice of employment but then again what other choices did he have. "Macduff won't be too pleased if I take up your offer," he said as Paddy unlocked the door and they entered the hallway, where the remembered scent of perfume mixed with the stink of cooking reached his nostrils.

One of the girls that Finn remembered as Pauline was just coming from the kitchen. Her scanty clothing proved that she was ready for her night's work. "Is that you, Finn?" she cried as she came across to stand in front of him. "What brings you back to this dump?" She gave Paddy a dig on the shoulder as she said this.

"He might come back and lend a hand. Why don't you try and persuade him, Paulie?" Paddy said as he walked to the end of the hall and went through the door into what Finn recalled was Vera's bedroom.

"Sure will," she said as she stroked her fingers down Finn's cheek. "We are sick of looking at his ugly mug, Finn. Could do with a good looker like you around this joint." Two other similarly attired women came from the kitchen and she called, "Come and help me talk this handsome bloke into coming back here."

Finn knew he had little choice in the matter, and this seemed to be a solution to his current problems. His shoulders and arm regularly ached a lot and even his hands hurt sometimes, so he knew it was only a matter of time before he would give up the fighting anyway. It was no lark for a bashed-about bloke like him. The girls settled him in the small room that he'd shared before with Paddy. They fussed about him before going off to prepare for the coming night. That was the part that displeased Finn more than anything—for a couple of them were barely out of their childhoods. But they seemed happy with their lot in life to have someone to care for them and a roof over their heads. Finn guessed that when you knew no other way of life you had to be satisfied with what you got. Much as he did himself. But with that thought came his self-disgust that he had let Esther, an angel, down. Knowing she deserved more than he could offer her came somewhat near to easing the pain within him.

As he predicted, Macduff was not pleased with him when he went to the hovel the Scot called home the next day to pick up his belongings. "Who do you think you are?" he blared. "I gave you a start when you were down and out chum, and you just want to throw it all away when things were going well for you."

Finn did not have the heart to tell the Scot that although he had made an honest living fist fighting, it was Macduff himself who had feathered his own nest. "My body can't take any more punches Macduff; you must know that I couldn't carry on much longer anyway."

"What about the big match I have lined up?" Macduff wailed like a stupid child.

"You'll find someone else to take my spot, and you know it. You have at least two blokes who can punch better than I can."

After a few more coarse words and shouting, Macduff let Finn walk out and into another phase of his life. It was a case of taking up where he left off. The girls treated him like a big brother and Paddy paid him well. When he lay his head down in the early hours of the day, sleep often evaded him as thoughts of Esther and how she was coping kept him awake.

Had her lost savings been returned, he wondered. There were a few times in the next couple of months when he thought seriously of returning to her, if only to ensure that all was going well with her and she was coping with a child to bring up alone. Only knowing how strong-willed she was stopped him from dashing off. Things hadn't changed that much anyway—he was still a useless pile of bones and always would be.

"What's up?" Pauline asked him on more than one occasion. "You ain't happy, are you Finn?"

"'Course I am. I've got all you lovely ladies to look after me. What more could I ask for?" he lied, for not one of them would replace his Esther.

"So you say, but it ain't true and we know it." Of course, they saw through his false show of happiness.

One afternoon in the first week of July he picked up the newspaper that lay on the kitchen table and a picture jumped out at him. "What's up?" Paddy asked when he saw Finn studying the page.

"Remember I told you about that cove who diddled my dear wife out of her inheritance?" Finn waved the paper. "Well, it seems he got bashed to death in the penitentiary." He read on down the page. "Looks like he did the dirty on more than one person and another of those that he stripped of their wealth got to him in prison when he was working outside, and gave him a good going over, and he never recovered."

"Looks like he got his comeuppance, eh?" Paddy took the page from Finn and read the article. "Didn't do any good for those he tricked though, for he died before telling them what happened to the loot." Paddy slapped the newspaper down. "Someone somewhere must know what he did with it. Perhaps it went back to the old country with the bloke you said took off back there."

"Well, no one is about to come forward now, are they?" This news from the past had shocked Finn. Often, he worried how Esther was faring. Would she accept him back, he wondered, should he ever have the nerve to front up at her door? Perhaps she had moved on by now and taken their child elsewhere. His worst nightmare was thinking she might have found a man more suitable than he to care for her. Could be she had fulfilled her wish and returned to England to seek out the relatives her parents left behind. The child could be about two or three months old by now, and he had no idea if it was wise to go on a sea voyage with one so young anyway.

"Ever think of seeking the missus out Finn, matey?" It was obvious that Paddy had seen the melancholy that gripped Finn when he dwelt on the past happenings.

Finn did not answer for a while as he contemplated doing such a thing. "Doubt she would want a loser like me back, Paddy. I'm not fit for any decent woman."

"Don't be so hard on yourself. Most of my ladies think you are the best." With a shrug he added, "But they ain't exactly decent women."

There were times when Finn considered Paddy's girls to be far better than some of the so-called posh ladies he had come upon in his time—types like Mona Franklin or Priscilla Clements. "It's all a silly idea anyway." Finn rose and went out to the yard behind the house. When all was said and done, what use was he anyway—always getting himself into strife. No, Esther was better off by far without him in her life. Yet still the ache inside him continued.

Business was blooming and Paddy's house had proved very successful. The girls were a lot better off than they ever were with Vera, who could be a nasty piece of work at times. Another couple of months went by with nothing changing. As the warmer days began to come in around the middle of September, Finn was awakened one afternoon by the cook, Dotty. Coming out of a deep sleep, for it had been a busy night, he sat up asking, "What is it?" as Dotty nudged him again.

"There's a young lass waiting in my kitchen. Says she wants to speak to you. Nice sort, not too fancy but speaks like a lady."

"A lady? What lady would be wanting to speak to me?" Finn glanced at the clock on the table by his bed to see that it was around two-o-clock.

"Dunno, but she's pretty. I wouldn't keep her waiting around if I were you. She might have second thoughts and disappear." Dotty went out.

Her words sunk in and hastily he climbed out of bed, pulled on a clean shirt and then his breeches and ran a comb through his unruly hair. Who on earth could be wanting to see him? A small niggle of something resembling excitement rumbled around in him before common sense took over. No way in this world would his Esther be here. A sense of urgency hit then as he pulled on his boots.

The soft rumble of voices came from behind the kitchen door and his hand shook as he opened it. His eyes saw the woman who never left his thoughts sitting at the rough old kitchen table, but his mind refused to believe it was really Esther sitting there. Her eyes met his as he stood there as if in a daze. The child in her arms was a girl if the dress she wore with fancy frills and the little matching bonnet on her head was proof.

When Esther said, "Hello Finn," his mouth dried up and like the idiot he considered himself to be, he simply nodded. "I hope it is not too much of an inconvenience me turning up like this." Her sweet voice was just as he remembered and heard in his dreams most nights.

Dotty left the room and Finn finally found the strength in his legs to go and sit down beside Esther at the table. The child held out a small hand as if to touch him and he took it in his own, marveling at its size and softness. "How did you find me?" Finn managed to get out.

"I saw Will one day at the marketplace and asked him if he was aware of your whereabouts. Seems he went in search of you and found that man Macduff who told him that you had ceased fighting for him. Will was planning on catching up with you one day, and on further questioning in the public house he garnered the information of your whereabouts. Of course, he was not certain if you were still here." With a small shrug she glanced about the room. "And as luck would have it you are. Still here, I mean." A small tremor in her voice told him that perhaps she was nervous.

"But why have you come here, Esther? This is not the sort of establishment for a lady to be seen in."

"I am tired of living without you, Finn. Our daughter, Fern, needs her Papa as she grows." She touched the hand not holding the babe's, and the soft caress sent shivers down to his feet.

"But I am not a fit person to be a father to any child, Esther. You must realise that I was a useless husband and would make an even more useless parent." Finn let go of the babe's hand and pushed his wayward hair back. Even as he said the words, he yearned to take Esther into his arms and hold her once more.

Without speaking she lifted the child and placed her in his arms. The girl stared up at Finn from eyes much like her Mama's, as if trying to fathom if she knew this man. As tears dampened his cheeks one of her tiny hands reached up and touched his chin. It was like being stroked by a feather. "That's your own opinion, Finn. I found you to be a good man and a splendid husband. Through no fault of your own, things went horribly wrong that day when you were attacked. Oh, and by the way, that stupid man got his chest back. It seems the thieves abandoned it after they took all its contents."

Having a sudden thought, he asked, "How did you come here today? Did you bring Danny Boy?"

"Yes, but do not worry. I was accompanied by a lad who works for my employer."

"Your employer?"

"Yes, I am still under the roof of Mr. and Mrs. Grace. Matilda has been like what my Papa would call a guardian angel. I would never be able to repay her for all the kindness she has shown me."

"You mean since I deserted you." The old self-revulsion returned. "You say you are under their roof, so that means you live with them?"

"It was her suggestion that I move in there and I still care for her three children as well as our daughter. I realise, Finn, that caring for children is the task that I am fit for. I enjoy my days and take pleasure in ensuring the little ones are taught manners as well as their lessons. Their eldest son has a tutor now."

"Did you hear that Reginald Smithson got his full deserts in prison?"

With a small nod she said, "Yes, and good riddance." Rising, she walked around the table until facing him. "I finally came to realise that half my inheritance was forever gone. Through my own stupidity, Finn, and nobody else's. You cannot take any blame for that incident, and I have put it behind me." She sat opposite him and reached across the table to take his hand. "I came here to beg you to come home with us. Fern seems to recognise you as her Papa, don't you see? It is not right for a child to grow up without both parents." Pausing, she sighed. "Would you consider my offer?"

Finn took a couple of deep breaths as he looked first at the child and then back to Esther. A vision of what life could be like with both of them flashed in front of him. This angel of a woman was prepared to accept him for what he was and had never asked more of him than that he stay at her side. "You are foolish to put so much faith in me, my dear woman. I have always thought that I will be beholden to you for seeing something in me that I cannot see in myself."

"So, you will come back with us?" She came back to sit beside him. "Mr. Grace rented the cottage we shared to another tenant after I moved to their home, but I have saved well since living under their roof and perhaps we could rent elsewhere."

"But what will I do, Esther? I must earn a wage, for I cannot be forever like a beggar. Things will never change as far as that is concerned."

Putting a hand up she said, "Let us worry about that once you come back with me. We could go elsewhere. There is nothing to stop us moving on." With a hand on his arm, she leant closer and placed a kiss on his chin. The child made a small gurgling sound that sounded very much like a laugh, and as Esther sat back, she too let out a laugh. "Please do not make me feel like a beggar."

All resistance left Finn as he pulled her close until the baby was gurgling even more when squashed between them. Perhaps she was giving him encouragement as, with a hand behind Esther's head, he covered her mouth with his own. How was he ever going to resist this woman's pleas? Fool she might be for wanting him in her life, but he would only ever see her as his saviour.

As Finn sat back, he brushed her hair away from her cheek. "How can I say no?" he said.

The door opened and Dotty bustled in, followed by Paddy. "I am sorry to disturb you two," she said. "But I have to make a start on dinner. The girls will be rising soon, and they are always hungry. Would you care to dine with us?"

"I would love to." Suddenly she said, "Oh my goodness, the lad who accompanied me here is still outside watching over my horse, so perhaps I had best be off home." Rising she bent to take the child from Finn's arms.

"I will come outside with you." Finn rose too. When they went out to the street, Danny Boy was dozing and the lad was asleep. He awoke with a start as Finn assisted Esther onto the bench and handed the babe to her.

"Shall I return for you tomorrow?" she asked with a touch of what Finn thought was nervousness.

"I will come to you," he said. Nodding to the lad, who flapped the reins, he then watched until the cart turned the corner.

Chapter Fourteen

When Esther came into the house after ensuring that her horse was comfortably settled down for the night, Matilda asked, "So how did your meeting go?"

Esther sighed as she sat on a chair opposite her and took off Fern's bonnet. "Well, I think. I now simply have to wait and see what Finn will decide to do."

"I have some news to relay also, Esther. You recall that I told you that my husband's uncle had recently died, well Mr. Grace has been assured that he is the chief beneficiary. Part of his legacy is a house in Launceston up north, and my husband wishes us to relocate there."

Chewing on her thumb tip, Esther nodded. "Of course, I did realise that if or when Finn joined me, we would need to find other accommodation. When do you think you will be going?"

"Well, if things do not work out to your satisfaction with your husband, Esther, we would have asked you to accompany us. But if you are sure he will join you, then it is imperative that you find other accommodation as quickly as possible, for my husband is already seeking out an agent to take care of selling this property. Be assured that I will miss you as I am sure the children will."

This news did not bother Esther overly, for she knew that there was no possibility of her travelling north with their family even if there was little chance of Finn joining her. "I will seek a cottage to rent if my husband decides not to join me, but if he does then I will see what he would like to do with the rest of his life." She was deeply disappointed when Finn did not wish her to return for him on the morrow but understood that he had no desire to leave Paddy straight away, for the man had kindly given him work when he so badly needed it. She left the Grace's address with him, for he said he would make his way to her, but now that the situation was changing, uncertainty filled her.

The next day, as Matilda had said, Mr. Grace was indeed showing the finer points of his home to an agent. Esther was on edge all morning, but the day wore on with no sign of Finn arriving at the door. As she prepared the Grace children and Fern for bed, she felt sick with nervousness. Try as she might, she could not rid herself of the fear that Finn would once again desert her. In that case she would need to find suitable employment with another family who needed care for their children. Now that she had a child of her own this would likely be more difficult, others would not be so lenient as Matilda.

Feeling unwell next morning after a sleep interrupted by thoughts of Finn, and when Mr. Grace had left for the day, Esther picked up his discarded newspaper. Matilda had advised that was probably a good place to start in her search for new employment. After glancing at the few advertisements for staff and finding none suitable for her needs, a name in a small notice caught her eye. The heading stated that a Mr. Ernest Blythe, formerly of Kensington, London, was seeking the whereabouts of any offspring of his brother Bernard Blythe.

Her heart did a somersault as she knew her Papa's name was Bernard, but was uncertain if he had any brothers. In fact, she had presumed he possessed no siblings, for she had never heard him mention his family other than the time she heard her parents discussing the family who apparently disowned her Papa.

Rising, Esther placed Fern in her basket on the floor and went in search of Matilda. She found her talking to her boys in the room set aside for George's lessons with his tutor. Looking up as Esther entered, she beckoned her over. "Are you all right my dear? You are looking pale. Has something upset you?" she asked.

Esther handed the newspaper to her and pointed to the notice. "I believe this man is my Papa's brother," she said, hearing the disbelief in her voice. "He is currently at a hotel in Hobart. Should I contact him?"

Matilda read the small article and then nodded. "Well, if you are certain that your Papa was named Bernard and your surname before marriage was Blythe, then by all means you should see him. Perhaps send a telegraph."

There was a small tap on the door and the maid came in. "Excuse me ma'am," she said. "There's a gent at the door asking after a Missus O'Connor. I told him there's no one here with that name and he said 'tis Esther he's after seeing."

"Oh, dear." Esther realised that the maid, of course, would not know her by any other name. Once again, her heart did a swift turn, as she realised it could only be one person. "Finn is here," she cried as all thought of her Papa's brother left her mind. Leaving the room at a run she went along the passage. Sure enough, Finn stood there with his hat in his hand. "You came." Esther ran into his arms.

"Of course, I came silly woman." He pulled her close and planted a kiss on her cheek. "I am sorry I could not get away sooner, but Paddy had to look for another to replace me."

"I understand. It is all right. You are here now. Come let us go and get your daughter." Taking him by the hand she led him into the dining room where Fern sat happily playing with her rag doll. Once he sat with Fern on his lap, she said, "I have some very interesting news. Do you recall I told you how I believed my parents left England under some sort of cloud?" She went on to explain the notice in the newspaper.

Matilda came in then with the page, and once Finn had read it, he said, "Would you like to go to Hobart and look this cove up?"

Esther nodded. "Matilda thinks I should send him a telegraph, so perhaps I will do that first. Also, there is more news to impart." Matilda left them alone then, and Esther went on to explain that regardless of what happened, they must now seek new accommodation.

"In that case perhaps we should do this straight away. We cannot expect your employers to provide us both with lodging here." He took her hand and pressed a kiss on it. "I want to be alone with you, dear wife, more than anything. Can you ever forgive me for deserting you?"

"Let us not dwell on past events, Finn. You are here now and as long as we are together and have our daughter with us, I shall be happy."

Later that night as they lay side by side in Esther's bed, Finn pulled her close and begged her forgiveness for his foolhardy ways. "As long as you promise me that you will always stay by my side from now on, I will forgive you anything," she vowed. It was as if the weeks of loneliness and unhappiness drifted away as he made love to her with tenderness and passion.

The following day the telegraph was sent to the man Esther hoped with all her heart was her uncle. Then it was just a matter of waiting for a response from him. Meanwhile, the Graces began packing for their move, so Finn's help was appreciated. Most of their furniture would be left in this house, for it seemed that their new residence contained everything they would need when they arrived.

Esther waited nervously for a response from Ernest Blythe. Would he possess any of his brother's finer traits? Her Papa was such a kind man as well as being very intelligent. His work in the field of medicine proved him to be a giant among men. Each day for the next three, she and Finn went to the telegraph office, and on the fourth day a reply arrived. Hardly able to contain her excitement Esther read, "I was pleased to hear from you. In three days' time, on Friday, I will arrive at The Bush Inn and await a visit from you. With warm regards from Ernest Blythe."

Trying not to read too much into his few words, she said, "He sounds to be a nice man does he not, Finn? I never expected him to be here in town, but thought we might have to travel to Hobart to meet him."

"Esther, you are a trusting person, so I hope for your sake that he is as nice as you want him to be." Finn caressed her cheek.

The house was in a flurry of activity as the Grace family finalized their packing. Esther continued to give lessons to the boys, for the tutor had already left. Their excitement was such that little in the way of real work was achieved. Esther knew she would miss the whole family very much, especially Matilda who had become like a sister to her. All this made her realise that she was putting perhaps too much hope in this new arrival.

When Friday arrived, Esther urged Finn to prepare Danny Boy as soon as breakfast was over. She fidgeted with her bonnet to such an extent that Matilda urged, "Calm yourself, dear girl. He is simply a man. I do not wish to dampen your enthusiasm, but it could turn out to be that he is not the uncle you expect him to be.”

With just a nod, Esther went out to join Finn. As Danny made his way through the busy morning bustle, her nervousness was such that Finn must have noticed for he also urged, “Calm yourself.”

As they went into the lounge of the hotel, a man who was sitting by a window rose and looked their way. Esther recognised him immediately, for he had her Papa’s chin and his honest eyes. Perhaps a few years younger than her Pa, his silvery hair was brushed back from a face that bore signs of weariness. As they neared, he held out a hand, and said, “I think you must be Esther, my brother’s daughter. I am so very pleased to make your acquaintance.”

“Yes, sir, I am Esther, and this is my husband, Finn.” She nodded Finn’s way. “Likewise, I am so happy to meet you. And may I say you are very much like my dear Papa.”

“Shall we sit?” He gestured to the vacant chairs near his. As he sat, Esther noticed that he seemed to have some difficulty moving. A cane rested on the arm of the chair testifying that it was likely he had a problem with perhaps his legs. “I would imagine you are inquisitive as to why I sought you out.”

"Oh yes. I cannot tell you how exciting it was to see your notice in the newspaper. And also, I am relieved that I actually looked at the newssheet, which is something I seldom do." Quickly she explained about their need to move.

That news seemed to interest him. "Well, first let me explain my visit to this part of the world, dear lady. My father died late last year. No, don't get distressed for me." He waved her words of sympathy aside and went on, "Bernard and I were the only offspring of our parents. I know how difficult our father made life for him when he decided to marry your mother." He shrugged. "Although deep down a good man, he could be very stubborn at times. I was never sure of his reasons at the time, but after his death my Mama told me that he thought the woman of his choice was not worthy of my brother. This opinion was based simply on some past feud between himself and your mother's family."

"I did know that Papa decided to relocate to the colonies because of this problem. My parents never disclosed the facts to me, but I did hear them discussing it once."

"I do hope that they found happiness with their new life and with each other."

"Oh yes, Papa was a very good doctor and Mama was proud of his achievements, as was I. Sadly, they died together in an unfortunate accident."

"Yes, this much I gleaned after arriving here in search of Bernard." He seemed to be deep in thought before continuing, "I was deeply sorry to hear of their passing and this made me more determined to find any offspring of theirs. So, it seems that you were an only child, is that right?"

"Yes, it is just me now." Esther felt sad but then asked, "So did your Mama travel with you?"

It was his turn to look downhearted. "No, and this is the true reason for my visit and search." He reached into a pocket inside his jacket and produced a folded sheet of paper. "Mama penned this shortly before she died a few months back. After explaining all that happened before and after Bernard left to go to his new bride, she said that I was to try and trace him using whatever means." He offered the note to her, saying, "She wrote this for him, so now it is yours."

Esther's hand shook as she took the page and unfolded it to read, "My darling son Bernard, it is with heavy heart that I pen this with the hope that you are living a full and happy life with the woman of your heart. I shall not be around for much longer and my deepest regret is that I never had the chance to find you and explain that it was your father's wish and his alone that forced you to leave beneath such a cloud of sadness. I so wish I could set eyes on you if only for one more time. I pray that you forgive me for allowing your Papa to treat you so dismally, and so hope that you have found a happy life with the woman of your choice. Sincerely yours, Mama."

Esther brushed at a tear that had fallen down her cheek. "And you came all this way to ensure he received this." Esther folded the page. "How Papa would have loved to hear that."

"There was another reason—perhaps a more important one." He looked from her to Finn, before saying, "You say you are leaving your current place of residence because the people you share it with have sold it and are moving on."

"Yes, I worked for the mistress as a nursemaid and teacher for her children— Finn and I have a daughter and Matilda Grace very kindly took me in when I needed a place to stay. Our child is with her at this moment." Esther hesitated as she looked to Finn, not wishing to say just why she needed a place to live at that time.

Saving her from making any explanation, Finn said, "I went away for a period, and that is why Esther moved there—because she did not wish to be alone."

All Ernest said to that was, "Ah, I see." Esther was not sure how much he saw of the truth in that, but he said no more, instead saying, "So you have a daughter. That is excellent news. Might I ask what you intend doing next in your lives? Have you decided on a new place to settle, or will you stay in this delightful town?"

"To be honest, we have made no definite decision. When I received your reply, I thought no further in my excitement." She smiled at Finn. "It is a decision we will make together."

"Of course, of course. Perhaps the news I have to impart will help you to make your decision easier." Reaching down, he brought a small satchel up onto his lap and opened it slowly. After reaching inside he brought out a scroll of paper and handed what appeared to be an official document to her. "On Mama's death our man who was handling our estate and all it entailed gave me that document. It clearly states that Mama's last wish was that Bernard or his offspring on the chance that he was sadly deceased, receive a fair share of the family wealth."

Esther's wits barely took in his words as she scanned the page. A figure stood out from the rest of the official written text and to her amazement it stated that her Papa, and as it stood now, she, was to receive the sum of fifteen thousand pounds. "But, but," she stammered. "You made this journey specially to deliver this to me in the case of Papa not being alive to receive it. What of you? This amount cannot be solely mine." She handed the document to Finn.

"Rest assured that it is. I am taken care of, do not fear. I have the house and estate too." With a shrug he added, "But it remains to be seen if I return there."

"You have no wife or family to go back to?" Esther asked when he had a look of sadness in his eyes as he said those words.

"No, there is nobody back there. Had I not traced you after finding out about Bernard's demise I would almost certainly have gone back." With another shrug he looked from her to Finn. "I rather like this town and may stay on here, at least for the foreseeable future."

That news pleased Esther for she liked this man. "What shall I call you? Would you like me to call you Uncle Ernest?" she asked eagerly.

"That would be very favorable, my dear Esther. I had a wife back home," he said, as if pondering on whether to tell her more or not.

"Oh, and what happened to her, Uncle Ernest?"

His mouth twisted in a small grimace before he admitted, "Sadly, my dear wife died while giving birth." A pause and then, "They both died. I think perhaps that she was past suitable childbearing years. The doctor said that there were many complications."

"Oh, I am so sorry to hear that." Esther wanted to give him a hug, but feared that would be too forward at this stage of their relationship. "Was your Mama there when this sad event happened?"

"No, and to be honest I welcomed the long journey here to give me time to grieve—and I was desperate to get away from the house and the memories." After a long pause he seemed to brighten as he said, "But now we both have family and I hope we can be happy together. And by the bye, you simply need to visit your banker and he can arrange the transfer of your wealth. I take it you do have a person you can trust. I would be happy to accompany you."

Esther thought momentarily of disclosing the stupid error of judgement she had made in trusting Reginald Smithson, but when she looked at Finn, his small shake of the head advised her to keep that knowledge to herself. "Yes, I had to visit the bank in Hobart to settle my affairs."

"Then I advise you to pay the manager a visit at the earliest opportunity." He sent a small wave to the maid who had just entered the room, saying, "Perhaps you can bring us some refreshment." With a nod she turned and left the room. "I hope you do not have to rush back to your daughter."

"No, she is well taken care of, if not by Mrs. Grace, then by her maid."

Once the maid had returned and poured tea for them, and offered almond biscuits, Ernest turned to Finn and asked, "So what is your intention, Finn? Are you in agreement with dear Esther here concerning your need to seek new pastures?"

Finn looked to Esther before saying, "I agree with whatever my dear wife decides. All I want from life is her happiness."

"Well spoken, young man. It is a sad fact of life that most men do not look to their wives for advice, but expect them to go along with their wishes whatever they may be. It has surprised me how prosperous the colony has become in such a short period." He looked thoughtful for a moment before adding, "I think, as I have decided to stay here, that I will seek a suitable house, perhaps a short distance from town."

As they made their way home, Esther said, "How strange life is, Finn. Just a short time ago we had no way of knowing what was in store for us, and now we can make a future for ourselves."

"All I pray, for your sake Esther, is that this man is totally honorable. I would hate to see you so downhearted as you were before. Please ensure that this legacy is genuine."

"I feel deep down that this new uncle of mine is truthful. Why else would he have sought out relatives, and what other reason could he have for coming to the other side of the world to find me?" Esther still had nervous butterflies flitting about inside her at the suddenness in her change of fortune. "Once I have spoken to the manager at the bank and the money has been safely transferred to my account, then we will decide how we wish to spend our lives."

Chapter Fifteen

Finn lifted a hand to shield his eyes from the sun as he looked across the meadow to where his two eldest children played near the kitchen door of their farmhouse. Fern was filled with excitement as she neared her fifth birthday and he could hear her explaining this to young Finlay, who although just two years younger than her, she still considered to be a baby. This despite the fact that their youngest, Essie, was still a babe at less than a year old.

With a sigh of satisfaction, he took a swig from his water bottle and then headed across to where they played beneath the shade of the back verandah. Fern jumped up and ran to meet him, calling, "Papa, come tell Finlay the story of the time you and Mama met."

"Not today. You've heard that tale many times and so has he. I will tell you another story." He sat on the bench beside the door and stretched his legs out in front of him, giving Finlay a helping hand as he scrambled onto his knee. "Did I tell you of the time when I was a silly lad living in London Town many years ago?" When they both shouted no, he continued, "Well, this was a long time before I met your Mama. I showed you on the map where that place is, didn't I? Yes, it is many miles across a very big ocean, that takes many weeks to cross in a sailing ship. So, this lad and I decided that we would try and steal a goat so that we could get ourselves some milk."

"That was naughty of you, Pa. Stealing is not good, is it?" Fern protested as she tapped his arm.

"Certainly not, but I did tell you that I was daft as a potato, did I not?" They both laughed at that. "And we were hungry. Life for us was nothing like yours. We have good old Mary the cow to give us fresh milk every day, don't we, but milk was hard to come by back then for lads like us. Your pa and his pal got themselves arrested, didn't they. And the funniest part of this story is that the animal we tried to steal was a Billy goat. And we all know that we can only get milk from girl goats and cows like Mary there yonder in the paddock, don't we?" There were oft times when Finn thought those far off days of his youth were dreams, or something his mind had conjured up. Or maybe they were real, and the life he lived nowadays was the dream.

"What did your Mama say about you being so bad? Did she cry and spank you?"

"Ah, Fern dear child, I never knew my Mama, I was not a lucky little 'un like you." Finn guessed this fact was far beyond the understanding of these young ones. He and Esther had discussed whether or not their children should ever learn of his early days and how he ended up being transported for his crime, and Finn decided that they should learn it all but only when they were old enough to understand how things were back then. Let them enjoy their peaceful life, far away from the realities of the cruel world.

"Where was your Papa then?" Fern frowned as she no doubt wondered at a world without a Mama to care for her.

"I expect he was off gallivanting somewhere, Fern girl." Finn gently put Finlay onto the ground and with a shrug rose, saying, "Enough tales for today. The work won't get done with me sitting about jabbering to you two all day, will it?"

"Can we ride on Danny Boy later, Papa?" she asked as she took Finlay by the hand.

Finn gave a wave to his shepherd who was coming towards him. "Yes, later. I now have to speak to old Zach about the sheep."

Their farm was not huge by any means, but Finn was not silly enough to think that he could ever manage it alone. Despite knowing nothing about farming, buying this place had been his idea. Zach was one of the three men who helped him. They didn't run a large flock but there were just enough sheep to bring in a fair income. Finn liked the sense of freedom it gave him.

Once Esther's inheritance was firmly in the bank those five years ago, she decided that she wished to go back to her dream of owning a store. Her Uncle Ernest was in favour of the idea, and he now managed the small emporium successfully in the main part of town with the assistance of his new wife, Margarita. This meant that Esther could enjoy the peace they shared out here away from the bustle of town, yet she could still have a say in what was bought and sold at the store.

"When should your uncle arrive for his visit?" Finn asked Esther later as they lay in their bed.

"He and Margarita should be here in time for Fern's birthday celebration tomorrow." Esther stroked his arm and leant over him. "He has some exciting news for you it seems."

"Hmm." Finn said no more. On one of his visits, Ernest had been more than a little interested in Finn's skimpy and uncertain past. It seemed that her uncle knew many men in positions of authority back in England who may have the power or knowledge to provide information on those transported to New South Wales over the years.

Baby Essie, who slept in her crib at the base of their bed, let out a cry and Esther rose to soothe her, so no more was said on the subject of Ernest's news but deep-down Finn felt a small twinge of something resembling excitement.

Their home was filled with childish chatter and yells the next morning as Fern and Finlay prepared for the coming celebration. When a carriage appeared at the other side of the farm gate, the cries grew. Esther was very pleased that the children had taken a liking to their uncle and also to his new wife. Margarita was a pleasant woman and said little. Finn thought her a little shy in company. A widow, she had a daughter who now resided in Hobart with her husband, so they had seen little of her.

Once the gifts had been presented to Fern and the children were now playing happily with the splendid new rocking horse brought by their uncle, the adults sat on the porch sipping cordial. Ernest set his glass down on the small table in front of him and said, "The acquaintance I mentioned who resides in London has sent me an interesting communication, Finn. You recall I said that he might be in a position to find out about the ships that were used for transportation?" Without waiting for a response, he continued, "After I advised him that you were likely sent to New South Wales around 1838, he went into the records pertaining to that year. It seems that most of those convicted were adults who faced long term sentences over fifteen to twenty years, but it was likely that one or two ships carried younger men who were mere lads so therefore garnered themselves lesser years in prison."

"But I do not know if I was listed under the name that I took for myself, so how can that be?"

"He passed on my queries to another person who was able to track down those born in Ireland and, as you said that it was likely your year of birth was 1823, this person then went into parish records. He came up with a woman who could possibly have been your mother."

Finn stared at him. "But that is impossible, sir, for I was taken from my mother as a baby by a Gypsy woman, so I was told."

Ernest waved a hand. "But what if that was a lie, Finn? The woman that you said took you to London as a small boy of around two years of age, was very likely the liar. After extensive searching on our behalf, this gentleman found that it was not uncommon for babies to be taken from their Irish mothers by members of the English gentry."

"Is it not exciting news, Finn," Esther said as she clapped her hands. "Perhaps you will now learn your true identity."

For so long he had thought of himself as Finn O'Connor and knowing that he might be someone else entirely was far too much for him to comprehend. "But how can I be sure that the facts this person is finding are true? It could be that I was not ever mentioned in the parish records that you speak of. What if my mother was the wandering gypsy that I was told I was stolen from by that English woman?"

"Ah, but that is probably where the lie began Finn, my good man. Truth, as far as can be understood, is that your father was the brother of this English woman. While in Ireland with the military, he met and let us say, took a fancy to a young Irish girl. Barely out of childhood it seems, she became pregnant with you. This was certainly not a rarity in those times. Unable to keep the boy child, she passed you over to the man's sister, who then took you to London. Whether the lass was coerced into this action is something we will never know, but it certainly seems a likelihood."

"So, you are telling me that I could now learn who my father is?" Barely able to take this news in, Finn took Esther's hand, while he pondered on this fact. Deep inside he knew that perhaps he did not wish to know the true identity of a man who would pass a baby over to his sister, and leave that boy to live a life where he did not know of his parents' part in this lie. "To be honest, Ernest, I would rather not know at this stage of my life."

That seemed to take Ernest by surprise. "But is it not better to have some idea of your roots? I feel certain that I would if placed in the same position."

"Ah, but that is where we differ, Ernest, for you are sure of your parentage whereas for all my life I have been unaware of the true facts. I had no doubts that I was born in Ireland and, of course, recall my time living in London with this family—who I must stress did not make my life easier, but from the time I ran away from them, I lived a life of petty crime. My name was even made up from some story about a man I read of, and that was simply because he was a hero of sorts and had the same hair colour as me it seems."

"Well, it is entirely your choice my fellow, but should you ever feel you need to know the name of the man who sired you, then it can be found."

They went on to discuss other things and as the afternoon wore on, Finn felt a sense of confusion. Should he learn of his roots if only for the sake of his children? After Ernest and

Margarita left and when the children were all tucked up in bed, Esther sat beside Finn beneath the back porch. "Are you certain you do not wish to know who your Papa was, Finn?" she asked of him.

With a shake of the head, he said, "It may eventuate that this man was not a man of honour, and perhaps I am better off thinking that my sire died. Even if it is all true and he forced himself on my Ma when she was little more than a girl, then I feel certain I would not wish to know a man with such little sense of right and wrong. And then, if it is true that he passed a baby over to his sister—who also had little love for the child, I feel I am better off living with the lies I have created. In the years that I lived with them, no man visited who seemed the least bit interested in my welfare. Do you not consider it strange that a man who sired me wanted no contact with me at all?"

Esther took his hand in hers and leant across to kiss him. "I suppose there is truth in that, Finn. If it is your wish, my love, then we will continue as we are." For a moment she looked at him deeply before asking, "You are content, aren't you?"

"Content just about covers all that I feel most of the time, dearest Esther. How could I not be, with a wife such as you at my side who has provided me with a family of my own? When I look back on the worst times in my life, I feel that never in this lifetime would I think that I could be this fortunate. That is why I prefer to live with the lie I created and just be happy that I am a person who, through no fault of his own, has become a man who could ask no more of life.”

“No more? In that case then how would you feel about having one more member of our family?”

Finn stood up and pulled her into his arms. Looking down at her with all the love in his heart he said, “If that means you are again with child, then that is wonderful news, my dear one.” Kissing her soundly he then whirled her around. Danny Boy whinnied loudly as if desiring to be part of this celebration. Hand in hand, Finn and Esther went across to where he stood by the fence of the field that he shared with their two other horses.

The End

Tricia McGill books also published by BWL Publishing Inc.

Settlers Series
Bk1. Mystic Mountains. Bk2. Distant
Mountains.
Bk3.Challenging Mountains. Bk4. Annie's
Choices.

Wild Heather Series
The Laird
Travis

Beneath Southern Skies Series:
Lonely Pride
A Dream for Lani
Leah in Love (and Trouble).

Challenge the Heart Series:
When Fate Decides
A Heart in Conflict
Kate's Dilemma.

Stand Alone
Remnants of Dreams
Amid the Stars
When Destiny Calls
Maddie and The Norseman
A Call Through Time
Powerful Destiny.
Laurel's Gift
Amethyst
Crying is for Babies
Sweet Bitterness.
For the Love of Faith

Award winning author Tricia McGill spent her early days in London, England, and moved to Australia many years ago, settling near Melbourne. The youngest in a large, loving family she was surrounded by avid readers, who encouraged her to read from an early age. Is it any wonder she became a writer. Although her published works cross sub-genres, romance is always at their heart.

Tricia's love of animals has always shown up in her books. Tricia devotes as much time and money as she can spare to supporting worldwide conservation groups and is passionate about supporting those who do all they can to preserve our wildlife for future generations. She also volunteers for a local community group that helps disabled adults and children to connect to the internet with provided computer equipment.